the perfect

indiscretion

(a jessie hunt psychological suspense—book 18)

blake pierce

D1568955

Blake Pierce

Blake Pierce is the USA Today bestselling author of the RILEY PAGE mystery series, which includes seventeen books. Blake Pierce is also the author of the MACKENZIE WHITE mystery series, comprising fourteen books; of the AVERY BLACK mystery series, comprising six books; of the KERI LOCKE mystery series, comprising five books; of the MAKING OF RILEY PAIGE mystery series, comprising six books; of the KATE WISE mystery series, comprising seven books; of the CHLOE FINE psychological suspense mystery, comprising six books; of the JESSE HUNT psychological suspense thriller series, comprising nineteen books; of the AU PAIR psychological suspense thriller series, comprising three books; of the ZOE PRIME mystery series, comprising six books; of the ADELE SHARP mystery series, comprising thirteen books, of the EUROPEAN VOYAGE cozy mystery series, comprising four books; of the new LAURA FROST FBI suspense thriller, comprising six books (and counting); of the new ELLA DARK FBI suspense thriller, comprising nine books (and counting); of the A YEAR IN EUROPE cozy mystery series, comprising nine books, of the AVA GOLD mystery series, comprising six books (and counting); and of the RACHEL GIFT mystery series, comprising six books (and counting).

An avid reader and lifelong fan of the mystery and thriller genres, Blake loves to hear from you, so please feel free to visit www.blakepierceauthor.com to learn more and stay in touch.

ALREADY TRAPPED (Book #3)
ALREADY MISSING (Book #4)
ALREADY DEAD (Book #5)
ALREADY TAKEN (Book #6)

EUROPEAN VOYAGE COZY MYSTERY SERIES
MURDER (AND BAKLAVA) (Book #1)
DEATH (AND APPLE STRUDEL) (Book #2)
CRIME (AND LAGER) (Book #3)
MISFORTUNE (AND GOUDA) (Book #4)
CALAMITY (AND A DANISH) (Book #5)
MAYHEM (AND HERRING) (Book #6)

ADELE SHARP MYSTERY SERIES
LEFT TO DIE (Book #1)
LEFT TO RUN (Book #2)
LEFT TO HIDE (Book #3)
LEFT TO KILL (Book #4)
LEFT TO MURDER (Book #5)
LEFT TO ENVY (Book #6)
LEFT TO LAPSE (Book #7)
LEFT TO VANISH (Book #8)
LEFT TO HUNT (Book #9)
LEFT TO FEAR (Book #10)
LEFT TO PREY (Book #11)
LEFT TO LURE (Book #12)
LEFT TO CRAVE (Book #13)

THE AU PAIR SERIES
ALMOST GONE (Book#1)
ALMOST LOST (Book #2)
ALMOST DEAD (Book #3)

ZOE PRIME MYSTERY SERIES
FACE OF DEATH (Book#1)
FACE OF MURDER (Book #2)
FACE OF FEAR (Book #3)
FACE OF MADNESS (Book #4)
FACE OF FURY (Book #5)
FACE OF DARKNESS (Book #6)

WATCHING (Book #1)
WAITING (Book #2)
LURING (Book #3)
TAKING (Book #4)
STALKING (Book #5)
KILLING (Book #6)

RILEY PAIGE MYSTERY SERIES
ONCE GONE (Book #1)
ONCE TAKEN (Book #2)
ONCE CRAVED (Book #3)
ONCE LURED (Book #4)
ONCE HUNTED (Book #5)
ONCE PINED (Book #6)
ONCE FORSAKEN (Book #7)
ONCE COLD (Book #8)
ONCE STALKED (Book #9)
ONCE LOST (Book #10)
ONCE BURIED (Book #11)
ONCE BOUND (Book #12)
ONCE TRAPPED (Book #13)
ONCE DORMANT (Book #14)
ONCE SHUNNED (Book #15)
ONCE MISSED (Book #16)
ONCE CHOSEN (Book #17)

MACKENZIE WHITE MYSTERY SERIES
BEFORE HE KILLS (Book #1)
BEFORE HE SEES (Book #2)
BEFORE HE COVETS (Book #3)
BEFORE HE TAKES (Book #4)
BEFORE HE NEEDS (Book #5)
BEFORE HE FEELS (Book #6)
BEFORE HE SINS (Book #7)
BEFORE HE HUNTS (Book #8)
BEFORE HE PREYS (Book #9)
BEFORE HE LONGS (Book #10)
BEFORE HE LAPSES (Book #11)
BEFORE HE ENVIES (Book #12)
BEFORE HE STALKS (Book #13)

BEFORE HE HARMS (Book #14)

AVERY BLACK MYSTERY SERIES
CAUSE TO KILL (Book #1)
CAUSE TO RUN (Book #2)
CAUSE TO HIDE (Book #3)
CAUSE TO FEAR (Book #4)
CAUSE TO SAVE (Book #5)
CAUSE TO DREAD (Book #6)

KERI LOCKE MYSTERY SERIES
A TRACE OF DEATH (Book #1)
A TRACE OF MURDER (Book #2)
A TRACE OF VICE (Book #3)
A TRACE OF CRIME (Book #4)
A TRACE OF HOPE (Book #5)

CHAPTER ONE

DeDe Albright thought that she had seen it all. But she was wrong. This time was different.

After spending fourteen years as a flight attendant, the last six of them working on private jets, she'd dealt with all kinds of behavior. On commercial flights, she'd broken up multiple mile-high lavatory hookups and even a few trysts in seats with just a blanket to hide what was going on underneath.

On several occasions, she had to zip-tie unruly passengers for everything from assaulting a flight attendant when she ran out of vegetarian meals to trying to break into the cockpit to have a "heart to heart" with the captain. She even got an air marshal to arrest a guy who was stealing all the mini-bottles of liquor directly from her service cart.

On private jets, the challenges were different. They included pampered, demanding passengers who felt they were entitled to scream at her when things weren't perfect. She dealt with spoiled kids who thought it might be fun to use seats as trampolines or attempt to smash cabin windows. And then there was the constant drinking and drugs.

The jet was stocked with enough alcohol to satisfy a fraternity party, but people often felt the need to supplement the refreshments. And everyone seemed to bring their preferred chemical enhancement. She remembered one time when a full baggie of cocaine dropped out of a guy's carry-on as he moved down the aisle and she had to chase him down to return it.

But none of that compared to the group on her current flight. The jet technically had the capacity for nineteen guests but this trip only had seven. Still, they more than made up for their limited numbers with their wildness. The journey from San Francisco to Los Angeles normally took only an hour; but they were taking an alternate route, curving out west over the Pacific Ocean in order to double the flight time and, therefore, the party time.

Everyone was taking full advantage of the extra hour and seemed unconcerned that it was barely after 10 a.m. on a Monday morning. She knew this outing was part of a fiftieth birthday bash, but even taking that into consideration, it seemed excessive.

Two men were sitting across from each other in plush, leather seats, doing lines of coke off the card table in front of them. Two women were engaged in some kind of tequila shot competition, complete with wrists, salt, and limes. Another guy, who had just finished dancing naked for his friends, was rifling through a baggie filled with multiple, brightly colored pills.

The sound system was blasting bass-heavy, house music and the lighting had been switched into "dance club" mode, which meant a darkened cabin, with a kaleidoscopic spray of rainbow lights and the occasional strobe thrown in for good measure. DeDe had developed a headache about twenty minutes into the flight and it had only gotten worse since.

The only positive was that no one seemed to need her for much so she moved to the front of the cabin, passing through the galley to the small, crew lavatory where she hoped to get two minutes of comparative quiet. She closed the door and took a few deep breaths.

Staring at herself in the mirror, she wondered how much longer she could keep doing this. She was thirty-six and starting to feel the impact of so many years at altitude. She was constantly sleep-deprived, her skin was suffering from the dry cabin air, and she knew at least six friends who'd gotten some kind of cancer in the last five years. All of them were younger than she was.

She had moved to private jets because she was sick of dealing with the cattle calls of commercial flights. But on days like this, she wondered if she'd made a mistake. She'd never dealt with an overdose or alcohol poisoning on a commercial flight but it seemed like a real possibility with this gang.

DeDe regrouped to go back out, reminding herself that there was only a half hour left in the flight. She opened the door to find a man standing right in front of her. It was the naked dancer guy who'd been fishing through the colorful pill baggie earlier. He was mostly dressed now. His eyes were red and as wild as his flyaway blond hair. He reeked of whiskey and weed.

"I'm sorry, sir," she said diplomatically. "You're welcome to use this lavatory but the passenger one in the back is much more spacious."

"I was actually hoping we could share this one," he slurred, stepping forward to block her path. "You know, christen it or something."

"That's all right, sir," she said, trying to be diplomatic. "We'll be landing soon and I need to help prepare the cabin."

2

"I promise it won't take that long," he mumbled, leaning in, wrapping his arms around her waist and squeezing her backside with both hands. She wanted to swat them away but the space was too tight for her to move. He was now in the bathroom with her, pressing her backward toward the mirror. She felt the panic rise in her chest. With all the noise and madness around them, if he closed and locked the door, it was possible that no one would hear her screams for help.

She was just about to resort to a knee to the groin when she heard a voice behind the man.

"Mr. Thacker," someone said loudly and firmly. "It's time to return to your seat."

The guy twisted around in the tight space. DeDe saw that the speaker was Anna De Luca, the other flight attendant. Young, pretty, and perpetually perky, Anna almost never raised her voice; but she was doing it now.

"You want to join us, baby?" he offered.

"Maybe another time," she said, less forcefully than before. "Come on, Mr. Thacker…Gareth, you don't want to be *that* guy, do you?"

Gareth seemed to consider the question, before turning back to DeDe and whispering in her ear.

"Let's consider this foreplay. I'll be back for more later."

Then he stepped back, maneuvered around to face the other way and stumbled past Anna, blowing her a kiss as he went by.

"You okay?" she asked, once he was out of earshot.

"He said that he's not finished," DeDe told her. "I'm really worried that he's going to try to corner me again. He was so aggressive. I'm thinking of alerting the captain. Maybe he can come back for a minute and scare the guy."

"You could do that," Anna said. "But it might make things worse. Thacker could try to get you fired. He's a major music producer. I've heard he can be really vindictive. I have another suggestion."

"What?"

"Talk to Edward Morse, the birthday boy; let him know how uncomfortable you are," Anna said. "This is his party and his flight. He's the one with liability. Plus, he's a big deal too. He doesn't want bad press. If he's afraid that you might sue him, he'll shut his buddy down fast. If he's not responsive, then you can still talk to Captain Graynamore."

The idea made sense. She didn't want to go to the nuclear option if she could avoid it. Her goal was to get off this flight without being assaulted or fired and if talking to the man paying for all of it could prevent either, it was worth a shot.

"Thanks, Anna," she said and made her way over to Morse, who was settled in the prime seat on the plane, on the right side, facing forward. It looked like all the partying had caught up to him and he'd drifted off. How he'd managed that with the craziness around him was beyond her.

As she got closer, she had second thoughts. Would waking him up to complain piss him off? She didn't want to alienate the very person whose help she needed. She stood over him, debating how to proceed. That's when she noticed the drool streaming down his chin from his open mouth. He looked more like he'd passed out than fallen asleep. Her mind flashed to her earlier concern about an overdose. Was it possible that one had finally happened?

Despite her apprehension, she gently tapped him on the shoulder.

"Mr. Morse," she said quietly, "I'm sorry to bother you but I need to speak with you."

He didn't respond so she shook his shoulder with a bit more force. His neck flopped lazily to the side, bending at what looked like an uncomfortable angle. He didn't seem bothered by it. In fact, as she looked more closely, he didn't seem to be responsive at all. He wasn't breathing.

"Wake up, Mr. Morse," she said loudly right into his ear as she shook his shoulder vigorously.

His whole body slumped to the side and his head hit the large window next to him hard, before lolling forward and slamming on the armrest. DeDe screamed.

Even with the pulsating music and the cacophony of voices, her voice rang out. Everyone looked over. Several of them saw the man and started screaming too. DeDe looked back to Anna, who quickly shut off the music and returned the lights to normal.

"Move aside," one of the men said, "I'm a doctor."

DeDe looked at him. Even in this horrifying moment, her brain took note of the irony that a man dedicated to keeping people healthy had a solid dusting of white powder in and around both nostrils. The doctor felt Morse's pulse as he rested his head against the man's chest. After a few seconds, he looked up and said in a surprisingly calm voice said, "Eddie's dead."

CHAPTER TWO

As soon as Jessie closed the garage door and entered her mid-Wilshire house, she sensed that something was off. Though it was 11 a.m., the place was suspiciously quiet. She knew her half-sister, Hannah—for whom she was guardian—was at school, but Ryan's shift at downtown's Central Station didn't start until noon. Usually, his presence meant sports on the TV and lots of noise as he blundered about the house. The silence was unsettling.

"Ryan," she announced, "I'm home."

His car was parked in the garage and he hadn't texted that his plans for the morning had changed, so she was sure he was around. But there was no answer. She tried not to overreact as she wandered into the kitchen, which was empty.

Just because nine months ago, he'd been stabbed in the chest and ended up in a coma for weeks, didn't mean that something was automatically wrong if he didn't reply right away. After all, with constant, aggressive rehabilitative therapy, he'd recovered over ninety percent of physical function and had been cleared to return to active duty last month.

"Ryan," she called out as she walked down the hall to their bedroom, doing her best to keep the apprehension out her voice, "you here?"

There was still no reply but she thought she could hear a scraping sound coming from the backyard. She continued that way cautiously, ignoring the urge to unholster her gun. Opening the door slowly, she peered outside.

There, standing on a flimsy looking ladder, trying to clean out the gutters, was the love of her life. He was sweating profusely and with his ear buds in, badly humming a song that she couldn't decipher. He was oblivious to her presence, which gave her a chance to drink him in without making him blush.

He hadn't completely regained the 200-pound, muscled physique that had defined him pre-coma, but he was working hard to get back there. And in his jeans and white t-shirt, he still looked like a model for some men's fitness magazine. His short black hair and dark skin both seemed to glow in the bright, late-morning sun. At this angle, she couldn't see his warm, brown eyes, but they were already permanent fixtures in her mind.

"Aren't you cold in just that t-shirt?" she shouted up to him. It was still February and the temperature was hovering in the mid-fifties.

He glanced around, confused at hearing something other than the music in his ears. When he saw her standing below him, he broke into a big grin and those soulful eyes flickered with joy. He turned off his music.

"What was that?" he asked.

"I was asking if you were cold."

"Nah," he said nonchalantly as he started down the ladder's steps. "Once I got going, I warmed up pretty quick. But I'm happy to risk a cool-down to take little break with you. How was class?"

She was about to answer when his shoe slipped on the ladder. He gripped the sides to prevent himself from falling but did so with such force that the ladder teetered to the side. As it toppled over, he leapt off in Jessie's direction, still a good five feet above the ground.

She rushed over to help break his fall, grabbing his torso and slowing his downward momentum. They collapsed in a heap on the grass with him on top of her. She took a second to determine if she was hurt and decided that she was none the worse for wear.

"You okay?" she asked, smiling up at her musky-scented fiancé.

"Uh-huh," Ryan said unconvincingly. He was wincing.

"What is it?"

"I think I rolled my right ankle when it hit the ground. I felt a tweak and it still kind of hurts."

Jessie fought the urge to ream him out for putting himself in a compromising situation.

"Let's get you up so we can see what we're dealing with," she told him.

Once she was upright, she helped pull him to his feet. He tried to put some pressure on his right foot. The sharp inhalation that came from him told her all was not well.

*

Ten minutes later, lying on the couch with his leg propped up and an icepack on his ankle, Ryan tried to convince her again.

"I think if I wrap it, I'll be fine."

"Absolutely not," she said, quickly going from irked to pissed off that he kept pushing. "You can't put any weight on your leg. There's no

6

way you can go into work as a detective if you're not mobile. You're lucky I'm not making you go to the emergency room."

"It's not that bad," he insisted. "I can do desk work."

"Or you can take the day to recover and avoid making things worse," she said firmly. "I promise I won't tell Captain Decker that you hurt yourself being a total idiot."

"What are you talking about?"

"Ryan Hernandez," she scolded, "I love you dearly so please take this in the spirit intended, but for a highly decorated detective, you can be a real dumbass. You decided that the ideal task to undertake while still not a hundred percent recovered from a stabbing/coma combo was to clean the gutters, using a tall ladder, when you're home alone? What if you'd hit your head when you fell? After all your hard work getting better, I don't want to come home to find you lying there like Humpty-Dumpty. Could you please not take unnecessary risks?"

"Jessie, I'm an LAPD detective. My entire life is an unnecessary risk."

She sighed.

"I'll be right back," she said as she walked to the kitchen. "I'm just going grab some water."

She didn't need the water as much as she needed a moment to regroup. She was annoyed but didn't want to kick him when he was down, both literally and figuratively. She also didn't want to get in an argument that would crush the high she was still riding from class. Though the seminar she taught at UCLA in forensic profiling had been over for a half-hour, she still felt giddy about how well it had gone. She'd held a lecture hall of over a hundred students rapt for ninety minutes as she detailed how she'd solved the murder of a young social media influencer that many of them followed.

Multiple students had come up to her in the last few days to tell her how impactful her course had been on them and how they planned to pursue a career in profiling and investigation because of her. A few of them had pleaded with her not to go.

That was because, two weeks ago, she'd committed to returning as a full-time consulting profiler for the LAPD when the winter quarter ended in a month. Her ostensible boss, Captain Roy Decker, had been begging her to come back since last year. After he offered her a sizable bump in pay, the freedom to stay in a consulting capacity rather than become an official employee, and assurances that she could still partner regularly with her fiancé, Detective Ryan Hernandez, she simply couldn't say no.

Kids who had been anticipating taking her class in the spring were disappointed, some aggressively so. UCLA had even assigned her a personal security guard after one (now former) student threatened to express his frustration through violence.

Still, the school had generously offered to let her return whenever she wanted, even if it was only for a quarter here or there. The reaction had been so positive that she was second-guessing her decision to leave. Was she more valuable solving today's crimes or preparing an army of profilers to unravel tomorrow's? Each option was rewarding and the idea of forgoing one for the other left her with a guilty pit in her stomach.

She had been planning to hash it out with Ryan when she got home. But as she gulped down the glass of water, she decided that this wasn't the ideal time to bring up her reservations about leaving UCLA to rejoin the force.

"Why don't I help you into the shower?" she suggested as she walked back over to him. "You're starting to smell a little ripe. You can use the shower seat from your invalid days, back when you were just out of the hospital."

He nodded and she helped him into the bedroom. While he got undressed, she grabbed the plastic seat from the walk-in closet. When she turned back around, she caught a glimpse of herself in the mirror. Dressed in slacks and a light sweater, she didn't look as frazzled as she felt.

Her shoulder-length brown hair was actually styled, a result of having enough time to properly get ready before her seminar this morning. Her green eyes were clear and refreshed. Her daily, early-morning, five-mile runs were paying off, as her lean, five-foot-ten frame looked strong and healthy.

In fact, until Ryan's mishap, they had both been making great progress on their fitness and rehabilitation goals. She hoped this setback was temporary as she set up the seat in the shower. She was just about to ease Ryan in there as well when her phone rang.

"It's Kat," she said.

"Go ahead and get it," Ryan insisted. "It might be important. I can hop my way to the shower."

He started doing it before she could protest. Not wanting to fight another personal autonomy battle, she didn't say anything. Instead, she smiled tightly and answered the phone.

"Hey Kat," she said as he disappeared into the bathroom and closed the door. "How are you doing? Back in town?"

"I'm good," Kat said. "But I've come and gone again. I drove back up to the mountains last night."

Katherine "Kat" Gentry, a private detective, was Jessie's best friend. She had gone up to the mountain resort town of Big Bear a couple of weeks ago with a dual purpose. A rich ski resort owner had hired her to determine if his wife was cheating on him. Conveniently, Kat's long-distance boyfriend, a Sheriff's deputy named Mitch, lived nearby in Lake Arrowhead.

As a result, she was able to work the case and see Mitch for a few days, without having to make the long drive from L.A. It had taken less than forty-eight hours for her to determine that the resort owner's wife was doing a *lot* of cheating. Once she handed over her report, she ended up spending the rest of the week hanging at Mitch's. After returning to L.A. for a few days, she'd apparently headed back to the mountains again.

"Are you back up there for a case?" Jessie asked. "Or are you just hunkering down in Mitch's love nest?"

"A little bit of both," Kat conceded, sounding embarrassed over the phone line. "But I have a big client back in L.A. who wants an out-of-town business partner tailed when he visits this weekend, so I'll definitely be back by then."

"Good," Jessie said, "Because we miss having you around."

"I'm sure you do. After all, I bet you've got wedding dresses and venues you want my opinion on."

"Actually," Jessie replied, realizing that now *she* had the embarrassed tone. "I've been slacking on that stuff a bit."

"Like how much?" Kat asked.

"Like, I haven't started yet," she answered. "I know this whole experience is supposed to be romantic and exciting. But every time I think about all the work involved, I get stressed. It seems so overwhelming. Picking a date, selecting a venue, deciding on guests, choosing invitations, even finding the right dress—the process is causing more anxiety than joy. Sometimes I think we should just get married at the courthouse and elope."

"Why don't you?" Kat asked, surprising her.

"What? Really?"

"Why not?" Kat said. "Ryan's been married once before, right? Maybe he's only participating in all the pomp and circumstance for your benefit. You should see. If you're both cool with it, you should go simple. This is supposed to be your day, Jessie. Whatever you do, it should make you happy, not fill you with anxiety. I mean who's going to complain—Hannah?"

"Complaining would require her to speak more than four words at any one time," Jessie replied.

"I thought things were getting better," Kat said. "Did something happen?"

"Not with me," Jessie explained, "with her therapist. Hannah told me that she had finally decided to come clean about…what happened with the Night Hunter. But when the moment of truth came, she couldn't pull the trigger. I asked her why and she couldn't explain it. She said she wanted to tell Dr. Lemmon the truth but when she tried, the words just wouldn't come out. Ever since then, she's been surlier than usual. It's like she's angry with herself and she's taking it out on me."

"That sounds about right," Kat said. "Has Dr. Lemmon said anything to you?"

"No," Jessie told her. "Even though Hannah's not quite eighteen yet, Lemmon is adhering to confidentiality rules as if she was. She obviously knows Hannah is hiding something huge. I guess she's hoping that eventually it will just feel too big to hold in any longer. And of course, it does no good for me to tell her. It has to come from Hannah."

She heard a door open and had a brief moment of panic wondering who was in her home before remembering that Hannah only had a half-day of school today.

"I have to go," she told Kat. "She just got home. But keep me in the loop on your mountain lover boy and let me know when you're back and able to hang out."

"Will do," Kat replied. "And good luck."

Jessie was just hanging up when Hannah, appeared in the doorway. She was hunched over, undercutting her normally tall, thin figure. Her blonde hair covered her green eyes, like she was trying to camouflage her face.

"I thought you had a class?" she said without preamble.

"Just got back," Jessie replied. "How was school?"

Hannah merely shrugged.

"You still have that appointment with Dr. Lemmon at two?" Jessie asked.

"Yes," Hannah replied. She looked like she might be about to say something more but then thought better of it, turned, and walked off silently. A few seconds later, Jessie heard her bedroom door slam shut.

"Nice catching up, little sis," Jessie muttered to herself. She was debating whether to go after her when her phone rang. By the bed, Ryan's did the same. Both caller IDs showed the same person: Captain Decker.

"Hi Captain," she said. "How are you on this fine morning?"

"Busy," he said gruffly. "I'm hoping you're not, because I have a case for you and Hernandez. Can you be here in twenty minutes?"

"Actually, Ryan hurt his ankle and he's limping. He needs to take a sick day."

"Okay, then you can come into the station solo," Decker said, neglecting to ask how his best detective got injured. "By the time you're here, I'll have a partner for you. I'll update you when you arrive."

Jessie sighed. She wasn't really in the mood to take on a case right now, especially with Ryan struggling. But she didn't have much of an excuse. She had finished her seminar and didn't have another one for a week. Her schedule was fairly open. And Decker usually only called her for help when the situation was significant.

"What can you tell me about the case?" she asked.

"I can tell you it's big," he said sharply, "and I can tell you to hurry!"

CHAPTER THREE

Jessie forced herself not to groan.

When she walked into Captain Decker's downtown Central Station at 11:30, he wasn't alone. Sitting in one of the two uncomfortable metal chairs across from his desk was Valentine.

Detective Susannah Valentine was the newest detective assigned to their squad, Homicide Special Section, an elite LAPD unit that focused on high profiles cases, many with intense media scrutiny, often involving multiple victims and serial killers. And according to others in the unit who had worked with her, she was good, if a little impulsive. But that didn't stop Jessie from disliking her.

She knew part of her distaste for the woman was unfair. Just because Valentine looked like a Sports Illustrated cover girl didn't mean that she couldn't be a good police detective. It wasn't her fault that her olive skin and hazel eyes appeared to glow, or that her thick hair cascaded down past her shoulders like a flickering, black waterfall. And she couldn't be held responsible for her perfectly symmetrical face or her sculpted body, which looked like it was designed specifically for bikinis.

Those were gifts Valentine hadn't chosen. What really irked Jessie was how aggressively the detective seemed to insert herself into investigations, often bulldozing over her more experienced colleagues to make her points or steal the spotlight.

And if she was being honest, there was one other thing that bothered Jessie. She didn't love how the woman interacted with Ryan, constantly laughing at his jokes, even the bad ones, tossing her hair around him, and generally getting into his personal space, the space reserved for Jessie.

"What's up?" she asked Decker, taking a seat next to Valentine and giving her a perfunctory smile. The woman was equally tight-lipped with hers.

"Thanks for getting here so quickly, Hunt," he said. "As you can see, you'll be partnering with Valentine on the case. This is your first time working together, isn't it?"

"Yes, Captain," she said noncommittally.

She might have been mistaken but Jessie thought that even behind his glasses, she saw a little twinkle in Decker's sharp, bird-like eyes. She wondered if he knew how she felt and was getting a kick out of pairing the two of them together. Her suspicions were raised further by the fact that the man looked positively jaunty.

He still had that wrinkly catcher's mitt of a face and the few remaining gray hairs on his head stubbornly refused to rest flat on his scalp. But unlike most days, he was almost smiling and his posture was borderline erect.

"Well, I don't think your first time partnering up will be boring," he said before launching in. "Less than thirty minutes ago a private jet landed at the Van Nuys airport with a dead passenger onboard. The pilot called it in as a possible overdose. CSU and the medical examiner's office are already there."

"If it's a suspected OD," Valentine asked, speaking for the first time since Jessie arrived, "why is Homicide Special Section involved? I thought HSS only handled high-profile murders."

"High profile *cases*," Decker corrected. "We don't know the details of this yet, but it's definitely high profile, which is why West Valley Division specifically requested our involvement. The dead passenger is Edward Morse. Ever heard of him?"

Jessie hadn't but apparently Valentine had.

"Edward Morse, as in Eddie Morse?" she asked. "The mega record executive who just signed a deal with that Middle Eastern venture capital firm for over 3 billion dollars?"

"That's the one," Decker confirmed. "Apparently Morse was returning from celebrating his fiftieth birthday on a small island that he'd rented for the weekend near the San Francisco Bay. So whether this was a heart attack, an overdose, or something more nefarious, we need to be thorough. This one checks all the boxes: rich, famous person dies during extravagant jet party returning from an island he rented. That's right up our alley. And even though Hunt over here just took down the leader of a powerful cult, that doesn't mean the knives aren't out for us. Our recent success has made HSS a target. We can't afford to have a public failure when everyone's watching. So stay focused out there."

"Anything else you can share, Captain?" Jessie asked.

"Not much," he said. "The officer in charge on the scene is Sergeant Dexter Stuckey. He'll have more for you when you arrive."

"Okay," Valentine said, standing up. "I just need ten minutes to get squared away. Then we can go."

13

"Make it two minutes," Decker barked at her, which Jessie didn't hate.

Valentine looked taken aback so he explained.

"All the people on that jet—each of whom could buy and sell us—are being held at the hangar until you interview them and permit them to leave. And from what I hear, they're getting pissy. You need to get going now."

*

The vibe in the car was awkward.

This was Jessie's first time alone with Susannah Valentine and she didn't know what to say. That's why she'd offered to drive—so she could pretend to be focused on the route. But even with the siren and flashing light on, it was taking a while to get to the airport, which was deep in the San Fernando Valley. After twenty five minutes of monosyllabic exchanges, she decided she had to take the initiative.

"Are you all settled in?" she asked.

"What?" Valentine asked, clearly confused.

"Back here in L.A.," Jessie clarified. "Weren't you in Santa Barbara until recently?"

"Yeah," Valentine said. "I left six weeks ago after two years with SBPD."

"And you came back because of family?" Jessie vaguely recalled.

"Right," Valentine said. "I worked patrol down here for almost five years but went north when a detective position opened up two years ago. Things were going pretty well. I had a few big case closures. But then my mom got sick. My dad passed away a while back and my brother moved to Miami years ago. She was alone, weak, and scared, so I didn't have much choice but to come back. I heard HSS had open positions and put in for one. I lucked out."

Jessie had heard some mention of this previously, but until now, hadn't really let it sink in.

"Do you live with her?" she asked.

"Yep, in the same house I grew up in. I sleep in my old room. She hadn't changed a thing. There are still Taylor Swift posters on the wall."

"How's she doing?" Jessie asked.

"Not great," Valentine said. "The cancer has spread. The doctors give her a few months. She's an eternal optimist, has lots of faith—goes to church every day. But I've secretly started looking at hospices.

14

With my schedule, I can't always be there for her and I can't take leave so soon after starting the job."

"You might be surprised," Jessie told her, her sympathy overruling her distaste for the woman. "Despite his gruff exterior, Captain Decker can be pretty understanding. I've had more than a few family crises, and he's always given me as much time as I need to deal with them. If you need to take a break, he won't hold it against you."

Valentine nodded but said nothing. Jessie let things lie and they remained silent for the last few minutes of the drive. When they arrived at the private hangar for Elite Aviation, the outfit that housed and serviced Morse's private jet, it was just after noon. They passed through security, parked in the covered lot, and entered the small terminal building that led to the apron and hangar. The building was impressive, with leather couches, an elaborate self-serve coffee station, and a small bar with bottles sitting out for anyone to make use of.

Jessie was still taking it all in when automatic doors opened and a short, muscular officer with thick black hair and a bushy mustache approached them. Jessie guessed that he was in his early forties. He looked like he could handle himself.

"Thanks for coming so quickly," he said, extending his hand to Jessie. "I'm Dexter Stuckey, Van Nuys Division."

Jessie's back involuntarily stiffened at the mention of Van Nuys Division.

"I thought West Valley Division was handling this, not Van Nuys," she said, shaking his hand uncomfortably.

Van Nuys was the same division where Sergeant Hank Costabile had worked. Until his arrest and conviction last year, Costabile was a powerful and corrupt cop, one who wasn't enthused when Jessie and Ryan discovered that his superior was sleeping with an underage porn actress. In fact, he was so displeased that he tried to have Jessie murdered.

Jessie had heard that even after he was put behind bars, he wanted vengeance. She'd also heard that some of his old compatriots in Van Nuys Division—Stuckey's division—might be willing to help him get it. The sergeant clearly noticed her reaction.

"I know what you're thinking, Ms. Hunt, but don't worry," he said. "First of all, I was only called in because no one from West Valley was available. There was an armed bank robbery in Encino about an hour ago. Now it's turned into a hostage situation and they're pulling almost everybody in on it."

"It's not the jurisdictional issue that has me concerned," Jessie said carefully.

"I get that," Stuckey replied, "and I don't blame you. But not everyone from Van Nuys Division is like Hank Costabile. We made a real effort to clean up after that embarrassment. I can't promise you that we've purged every bad apple, but we're working on it. And you've got nothing to fear from me. Once I was assigned to this case, I was the one who recommended we bring you in."

"What's this all about?" Valentine asked, confused. She'd been in Santa Barbara when the whole thing went down and clearly didn't get the reference. Stuckey turned to her.

"Sorry about that, Detective Valentine," he said, shaking her hand as well. "I didn't mean to be rude. Let's just say that until recently, this division didn't have the most sterling reputation. Your partner forced some changes that a few folks still resent. I'm sure she can fill you in on the details later. But for now, I'd like to take you to the hangar where we're holding the passengers and the plane. This group is filled with some colorful characters, all of whom are getting antsy. The sooner you can start questioning them, the better off everyone will be. Will you please follow me?"

As he led the way, Jessie saw the CSU and medical examiner vans parked by a massive hangar. Realizing she was about to be doused in a fire hose of evidence and witness statements, she quickly texted Jamil Winslow, the brilliant HSS police researcher who had proved invaluable to her on so many occasions.

Typing as quickly as she could, she made a request that she would have thought of earlier if she hadn't been driving: *need everything you can find of note on record exec Eddie Morse. Will call later.* She included Valentine in the group and hit "send."

The text had just gone through when Sergeant Stuckey stopped at the door to the large hangar. He turned back to them, and spoke with trepidation in his voice.

"Get ready for the circus."

Then he opened the door.

CHAPTER FOUR

The first thing Jessie noticed was the plane.

How could she not? It was stunning. Long and sleek, it was white with a blue stripe along its length, and looked to be larger than some of those puddle jumper commercial planes. It was so shiny that it almost seemed to glisten and its image reflected on the cream-colored hangar floor, which also gleamed pristinely. She was about to ask what kind of plane it was when she heard someone yell from somewhere she couldn't identify near the back of the hangar.

"My husband will sue you into the poorhouse!" a female voice screeched.

"What was *that*?" Valentine demanded.

"That," Sergeant Stuckey said with a sigh, "is one of the people you'll have the pleasure of questioning momentarily. We're holding them in a series of separate offices that line the back of the hangar over there. Would you like to start with them or see the body first?"

"Body," Jessie and Valentine said in unison.

"What a shocker," he replied, pulling out his radio. "Not that I blame you. Morse is still on the plane. Let me just get the facility superintendent. That way if you have any questions about the aircraft, he can help you out."

He walked them to the retractable stairway as he called for the superintendent to join them. They waited at the bottom of the stairs. A moment later, a heavyset guy in slacks, a shirt, and tie barreled through a nearby door. He looked young, maybe in his mid-twenties, with curly brown hair and navy-framed glasses. He was sweating profusely, even on a brisk February day, but he seemed oblivious, bouncing over to them with impressive energy.

"Hi ladies," he said enthusiastically. "Sorry for the delay. As you can imagine, it's been a little crazy here in the last hour. I'm Jonah Navasky, the facility superintendent. I'm here to offer whatever help you need to expedite this situation. Can I invite you onboard?"

"Thanks very much, Mr. Navasky," Valentine said, clearly as overwhelmed by the man's liveliness as Jessie was.

"Please call me Jonah, Detective Valentine" he said as he led the way up the stairs. "As I already told Sergeant Stuckey, it's an honor to work with the LAPD. And of course, everyone knows about your exploits, Ms. Hunt."

Once he led them up the stairs to the jet entrance, he stepped aside and beckoned for them to step inside. Valentine went first and Jessie followed. She tried not to let her jaw drop to the floor. They were at the front, near the cockpit, which looked more advanced than anything she'd seen on a commercial flight.

To get to the main cabin, they had to pass through a galley, complete with a long granite counter, a glassware cabinet, a microwave and full oven, and even a divan.

"What kind of plane is this?" she asked.

"It's the Gulfstream G700," Jonah told her. "It's the company's newest model, not yet available for purchase by the public."

"Then how was it able to be flown this morning?" Valentine asked.

"That's a good question," Navasky said. "This plane is owned by a Qatari group. They bought a fleet of them for $75 million each. The rest are currently in the Middle East or still being built. But the group lent this one to Mr. Morse after their investment in his company, as a kind of birthday gift."

"I bet they're regretting that today," Valentine said. She stopped at a curtain, which was pulled across, blocking access to the main cabin. She looked back at Jessie to see if she objected to opening it. Jessie nodded to go ahead.

Valentine pulled it back to reveal a large, crowded cabin. Mixed in among the plush seats, the full bed in the very back, the sofa, the card table, and the giant TV monitor, Jessie counted three CSU techs and two folks from the medical examiner's office, one of whom was standing in front of the seat where she suspected Morse was still sitting. They all looked back toward the galley and the person in front of Morse's seat turned around. Behind her, Jessie could see Morse's body, slumped awkwardly to the right.

In his current condition, it was hard to draw too many conclusions about the man. Though his body was contorted, it looked like he was in good shape for a guy who had just turned fifty. She suspected that he may have dyed his brown hair, which was devoid of any gray at all. Even after a weekend of partying he was clean-shaven.

"Detective Valentine, Ms. Hunt," Sergeant Stuckey said from behind them, "this is assistant medical examiner Fiona Guglia."

The woman, tall, thin, and severe looking, gave them a curt nod.

"We're basically done here," she said without greeting, her tone patrician and borderline condescending. "The CSU folks can fill you in on what they found or I can go first if you prefer."

"Let's hear from you," Valentine said, not asking for Jessie's opinion. "Was it a heart attack, an overdose, or an overdose-induced heart attack?"

"Actually," Guglia said. "I don't think it's any of those. We can't say definitively until we get to the lab, but it appears that this man was poisoned."

"I'm sorry, what?" Valentine said, shocked. "We were led to believe this guy's death was result of partying too hard."

"I suspect that was what you were intended to believe," Guglia said patronizingly. "His preliminary blood work doesn't suggest a heart attack or stroke. I did an initial tox screen and found a massive concentration of diacetylmorphine—that's heroin—in his system, far too high to suggest an overdose. No one could intentionally consume that amount. It's enough to kill a large horse. Someone had to have given it to him without his knowledge."

Jessie and Valentine exchanged stunned glances. What they thought was an overdose had just morphed into a potential murder. Jessie finally recovered enough to reply.

"How?" she asked.

"Possibly with this," she answered, pointing at the empty glass by his seat. "It has heroin residue inside. We're also going to test an empty flask that was found in his jacket. It's conceivable that the flask was poisoned earlier and he unknowingly poured the tainted drink into the glass."

"You can't do a preliminary test on it now?" Valentine asked.

"I want to do that under lab conditions," Guglia told her. "Getting a sample from it will be more challenging than the glass. Regardless, I suspect that either prior to this flight, or more likely during it, someone mixed a lethal amount of it in his drink. At the concentration involved, it would only have taken a few gulps to do him in, and the glass was empty."

"So just to make sure that we understand you clearly amid all the talk of blood work and toxicity," Jessie said, "It's your medical opinion that this death was not just a terrible, self-administered poisoning by a guy who was probably already drunk and high. You think he was murdered."

"I'm quite confident," Guglia said.

"Maybe you could have led with that," Valentine noted sharply.

19

"I didn't want to step on toes," the woman replied unconvincingly.

Jessie didn't want this to turn into a battle of wills so she short-circuited the dispute with another question.

"You said you think the poisoning 'more likely' occurred on the flight rather than prior to it," she noted. "Isn't it possible that the flask was poisoned earlier and he just happened to drink it on the flight?"

Guglia shrugged noncommittally.

"I can't be sure of anything until we test the flask," she admitted. "But sneaking a large quantity of powdered heroin into a narrow-mouthed flask would be challenging, especially under duress, if the perpetrator was worried about being discovered. It could be done but dropping it directly into his glass during what appears to have been a wild party seems much easier."

Jessie didn't disagree, though she could see that Valentine was irked that a medical examiner was veering into cop territory.

"In addition," Guglia said, oblivious to the detective's irritation, "Mr. Morse was clearly fond of his chemicals. It seems unlikely that he would have held off on consuming what was in the flask until he'd been on board for over an hour. If he drank from that flask and it was poisoned, he'd have been dead in less than fifteen minutes. Do *you* think he could have held off drinking from it for an hour?"

Out of the corner of her eye, Jessie saw Valentine open her mouth, almost certainly to chastise the medical examiner for veering out of her lane again. She jumped in first, before the detective said as much.

"Wouldn't he have been able to taste that amount of heroin in his drink?" she asked.

"Sure, if he was taking sips and generally alert," Guglia said. "But if he was taking big gulps or doing shots, probably not. Add in the fact that he was likely bombed before he started drinking it and I doubt he'd notice much of anything."

That answer made sense. Even Valentine didn't object to it. Jessie decided to move on before the detective changed her mind.

"Anything CSU wants to add?" she asked.

"There's not much to tell," offered a young man who stepped forward. "There are fingerprints everywhere, not a shock in a confined space like this, but only Morse's prints are on the glass."

"That's not surprising," Jonah Navasky piped in. "While flight attendants offer drink service, passengers are also able to serve themselves if they prefer. It's certainly possible that he just poured himself something. In fact, it sounds like that was Mr. Morse's thing."

"Good to know," Jessie said, before turning back to the CSU tech. "Anything else?"

"We'll have a full DNA analysis later," he continued, "but I wouldn't expect it to help much. This place is a flying petri dish, awash in every drug you can imagine. It's clear the passengers tried to do a little cleanup once they knew police would be coming on the plane, but we found residue of at least half a dozen chemicals that would make your head spin."

"I don't suppose there are any cameras onboard?" Jessie asked.

"I'll take that one," Sergeant Stuckey volunteered. "There are, but it won't surprise you to learn that Morse had them all turned off for the flight. I guess he didn't want any record of the activities taking place in the friendly skies."

"So," Jessie said, "we have a murder, very possibly committed in the presence of multiple other people, some oblivious, others high. We have almost nothing in the way of physical evidence to tie anyone to the crime. And we have multiple suspects and witnesses, all incentivized to keep their mouths shut because they were engaged in all kinds of illicit behavior. Do I have it about right?"

"Sounds on the money to me," Sergeant Stuckey agreed.

Jessie turned to Valentine.

"Then I guess we have some interviews to conduct."

CHAPTER FIVE

"I should warn you," Stuckey said as they entered Jonah Navasky's office, which was set just off the hangar. "Some of these people are still pretty high."

"Wonderful," Jessie said. "That should make for coherent interrogations. Who have we got here?"

She, Valentine, Stuckey, and Navasky were looking at a bank of small, fuzzy monitors that showed multiple other offices. In each one were several people. Stuckey pointed at the screens.

"We tried to keep everyone separated as much as possible, but there are only so many offices so we had to double up in some cases. We're keeping at least one officer in with them to prevent inappropriate discussion or attempts to compare recollections."

"Normally, we only turn on these cameras at night for security purposes," Navasky said quickly. "I don't want you to think we regularly surveil our clients."

"Don't worry, Mr. Navasky," Valentine assured him. "Your security choices are not at the top of our priority list right now. Unless you were on that plane when Eddie Morse died, you can breathe easy. Who are we looking at?"

"The big office has the pilots and flight attendants," Sergeant Stuckey said, pointing at the appropriate screen. "That's Captain Harry Graynamore. He was in the Navy, then a commercial airline pilot for fourteen years. He's been flying private jets for the last eight. His co-pilot, Ned Waturi, did ten years commercial before coming over to private four years ago. Both the flight attendants followed the same path. The senior attendant, Deirdre Albright, is thirty-six; she found the body. The junior attendant is Anna De Luca, twenty-seven. As you'd expect, none of them have been a problem. They answered all our preliminary questions without complaint and have been waiting patiently ever since. I wish I could say the same for the others."

"Who was the one screaming about the lawsuit?" Valentine asked.

"That'd be Vivien Baldwin," Stuckey said, tapping the screen in question. "Her husband, Joseph, really is a lawyer, and apparently Morse's business partner too. That's him pacing."

"And the others?" Jessie asked, indicating another screen.

"That pair is Dr. and Mrs. Glenn and Lucy Ward. He's the one who verified that Morse was dead after the flight attendant first noticed. The last office is Gareth Thacker and Patricia Morse. He's some big-time music producer that Morse worked with."

"I've heard of him," Valentine said. "He's a hit machine."

"We wanted to give Morse a private room," Stuckey said, "but Thacker was unrelentingly obnoxious. The only way to get him to temper it even a little was to put him with the dead man's wife. He's quieted down a bit since then."

"Okay," Jessie said. "That gives us ten witnesses, one of whom is likely a killer. What do you say, Valentine—shall we split this up to save time?"

"Sure," the detective replied. "Mr. Navasky, are you able to record the interviews?"

"The video isn't a problem," he said. "But there's no audio so I don't know how much good it'll do."

"We'll just have to use our phones, along with pen and paper," Jessie said, sounding brusquer than she'd intended. Valentine didn't object, or say anything at all for that matter.

"Then I guess you better get started," Stuckey advised. "I'm worried that with everything they consumed on that flight, a few of these folks might pass out soon."

*

Jessie started with the widow.

Patricia Morse was in bad shape. It was apparent that under normal circumstances, she was an attractive woman, but the combination of grief, the comedown from whatever she was on, and the stress of being questioned wasn't doing her any favors. According to the info Stuckey had given her, she was thirty-eight, over a decade younger than her husband. But right now, she looked a good decade older than that.

Her bleached blonde hair was frizzy, as if she'd been rubbing it repeatedly. Her eyes were red and her mascara had run where she'd been crying. For obvious reasons, she hadn't thought to check a mirror.

Jessie glanced out the office window. Gareth Thacker had been temporarily relocated to an unoccupied part of the hangar. She wanted to make sure the officer assigned to him had moved him far enough away that he couldn't hear their discussion. Then she returned her attention to Morse. She'd already offered condolences for the woman's loss, so she decided to dive in.

"Some of these questions might be difficult to hear, but the more direct and complete your answers, the faster we can resolve the circumstances of your husband's death," Jessie said. She and Valentine had agreed not to reveal that Eddie Morse's death was likely not an accidental overdose or heart attack, but a murder. The less that these folks knew, the less defensive they would hopefully be.

"I understand," Morse said, her voice already quavering.

"So your husband rented out an entire island for his birthday bash. Is that right?"

"It's not as ostentatious as it sounds," Morse told her, dabbing at her eyes. "It's a tiny spot called Eastern Sister Island near the San Francisco Bay, with a working lighthouse and a bed and breakfast. There are only four or five rooms. So if you rent out all the rooms for the weekend, you've technically rented out the whole island."

"I see," Jessie said, still impressed. "And how did he come to choose the folks that joined you for the weekend?"

Morse sighed heavily, as if the burden of answering the question might be too much. After a few seconds, she replied.

"Joe Baldwin is…was Eddie's business partner. He ran the business side of their company, Eddie Records. We've been friends with him and Vivien for years. Eddie has known Glenn Ward since they were freshman roommates at Oberlin. He's one of his oldest friends. He was also Eddie's personal physician. Lucy's his wife. She went to college with them too. They all moved out to L.A. together. Eddie was best man at their wedding."

"What about him?' Jessie asked, nodding in Thacker's direction.

"Gareth is the company's top producer," Morse said disdainfully. "He's also a world class jerk. Eddie didn't really want to invite him but he'd heard rumors that Gareth might be considering leaving the label so he figured he could use the weekend to grease the wheels a little."

"Did it work?" Jessie asked.

"Eddie told me that it did," Morse said. "But I suspect that's all out the window now."

"Were there any major arguments over the course of the weekend, Mrs. Morse?" Jessie asked as casually as she could. "Anyone leave the island upset?"

"Are you kidding?" the woman asked, coming close to laughing despite the situation. "I don't think there's ever been an outing with this group that didn't include multiple blowouts, screaming matches, or threats to end business or personal relationships. It's kind of our thing."

"Even between you and Eddie?"

"Especially between me and Eddie," Morse replied, her voice thick with emotion. "It's part of what kept things spicy between us."

Discussing the nature of their relationship seemed to push Patricia Morse over the edge and she collapsed into tears. Jessie tried to calm her down but it was no use. She motioned for a female officer to come in the room and stepped out. She wasn't going to get anything useful out of the woman, at least not right now.

She allowed herself a moment to take stock. Not only were there no cameras, no real alibis, and hardly any physical evidence to speak of for this case, but now the victim's own widow was admitting that every passenger on that plane, including herself, was a credible suspect.

"This is going *great*," she muttered under her breath.

CHAPTER SIX

Jessie was getting frustrated.

Her separate interviews with Joe and Vivien Baldwin had proven equally fruitless. Joe's answers were all boilerplate attorney-speak and Vivien seemed more focused on blaming the LAPD for "incarcerating" her in the hangar office than shedding light on what had happened.

The captain, a gentlemanly, fifty-three-year-old, silver fox named Harry Graynamore, was gracious, but as he was in the cockpit the entire flight, he didn't have much information to offer.

Last on her half of the witness list was Deirdre Albright, the flight attendant who'd initially discovered something was wrong with Eddie Morse. Jessie entered the office where Albright was waiting with the rest of the crew.

"May I speak with you privately, Ms. Albright?" she asked.

The woman nodded and got up to follow her. As she did, Jessie studied her. Much like Patricia Morse, she looked older than her age. But unlike Morse, Jessie doubted it was temporary for her.

Though she was attractive, it was clear that years of long hours on her feet at altitude had taken a toll. Her skin looked haggard. Her black hair appeared dull and brittle. Her whole body seemed to droop, as if she had a small leak and was slowly deflating. And from the frazzled look on her face, Jessie didn't hold out much hope that she'd be useful.

Jessie led her to a far corner of the hangar, away from anyone else, and indicated for her to take a seat in the folding chair that had been set up for the other crew interviews.

"Sorry for the accommodations," she said. "We're making do with what we have."

"That's okay," Albright said. "But I'm not sure why we're doing this here instead of at the police station."

"To be honest, Ms. Albright, it's because we weren't confident that we'd be able to get full statements from some of these people once we remove them from this location. I'm not impugning you or your colleagues. You've been very cooperative. But unfortunately, if we let the crew go to the station, the passengers will demand the same, which could get messy."

"Because they're not being forthcoming?" she asked.

"Not so far," Jessie said. "But we're hoping to change that. Do you have any idea why they might be reluctant to talk about the events surrounding Mr. Morse's death?"

"I'm guessing it has something to with all the partying they were doing."

"Can you be more specific?"

Albright nodded reluctantly.

"Well, I'm sure it's no secret that a lot of drugs were consumed," she said. "From the minute they boarded the jet, they were snorting and smoking everything in sight. There was also lots of drinking. It seemed like they were all in a race to see who could get messed up the fastest. At one point there was some half-naked dancing going on in the aisle. One passenger stripped down completely and started dancing in his seat."

"I'm assuming that was Mr. Thacker," Jessie prompted. She'd already heard that it was him from both the Baldwins.

"Yes," Albright said, casting her eyes downward. "I only wish he would have stuck to that."

"What do you mean?" Jessie wanted to know.

She hesitated briefly, but then seemed to make a decision to say her piece.

"At one point, he cornered me in the front lavatory and forcefully propositioned me. I was concerned that it might get physical. Luckily, Anna, the other flight attendant, came across us and smoothed things over."

"I'm sorry that happened to you," Jessie said, trying to keep her voice even. She didn't want her own outrage at what Albright had described to influence anything the woman might share going forward. Nor did Jessie want Albright to know that she was already calculating the odds that Gareth Thacker might be responsible for more than an alleged assault.

"Yeah, it was pretty scary," she admitted. "That's actually how I found out about Mr. Morse's…condition. I was going to tell Captain Graynamore what happened, but Anna suggested I might have more success keeping Thacker away from me if I told the person who'd booked the flight. She thought he might be afraid of a lawsuit and would shut Thacker down to protect himself."

"So you went to speak to him right away?"

"Yes," Albright said. "It looked like he might be passed out. But when I shook him, he collapsed over on his side. He was drooling and the way his body bent, I knew something was wrong."

She closed her eyes as if to shut out the memory.

"What happened after that?" Jessie asked.

"Then his doctor friend checked him out and said he was dead. Once that happened, all hell broke loose. Mrs. Morse started wailing. Some of the others tried to console her. Captain Graynamore announced that we would be expediting our arrival to the airport, where the police would meet us. That's when things changed. People started wiping the drugs off the tables. I saw Thacker take his satchel to the rear lavatory. I'm pretty sure he was dumping all his stuff in the toilet, which was pointless because it's all still down there if anyone needed to find it."

"Did you see anyone get into a dispute with Edward Morse, or notice him treat someone else poorly?" Jessie asked, making a mental note to have the toilet holding tank checked later. It might not be proof of murder but having something to use against Thacker later couldn't hurt.

Albright thought about it for a moment.

"I don't remember anything like that," she said. "He was pretty raucous but no more than anyone else. It was so crazy with all the yelling and the music blaring and the lights flashing that I was just trying to keep my head above water. I wasn't really paying that close of attention."

Jessie debated whether to ask the next question, but as this was the last of her interviews, she decided to go ahead. It's not like Albright could warn anyone else about what was coming.

"Did you serve Mr. Morse any drinks during the flight?"

"I offered everyone coffee," she replied. "Some took it but not him. He was focused on the booze, which he poured himself. For a while, he and some of the others were even trading a bottle back and forth."

"Did you see anyone else pour a drink for him?"

Albright shook her head.

"To be honest, with everything going on, that wasn't something I focused on. Why?"

"I'm just trying to get a fuller picture of events," Jessie lied. "I think that will do for now. You can go back to the office, but please don't discuss anything we talked about with your co-workers."

"Of course not," Albright assured her, though Jessie was certain that she was lying too.

As the flight attendant made the long walk back across the hangar, Jessie plopped down in the chair that the flight attendant had been occupying. With her interviews done for now, she tried to assemble a coherent picture in her mind.

When it came to the big things, everyone (except Captain Graynamore, who was never in the main cabin) mostly agreed. Lots of drugs were consumed. Gareth Thacker—who was at the very least a potential sexual predator, and maybe more— danced naked. Deirdre Albright discovered the body. Dr. Glenn Ward confirmed he was dead. And all the passengers were generally on the same page about the events prior to the flight, including their time on the island and the interpersonal volatility all weekend.

It was the details she couldn't get any clarity on. Who exactly fought with whom and when? How many chemicals did Eddie Morse consume? When did people last notice him conscious?

It didn't help that most of the people on the trip were either getting high or coming down from a high all weekend long or that the flight sounded like a mid-air rave. Amazingly, these people might be able to credibly use their altered states as excuses to avoid providing alibis or confirmable testimony.

The whole situation was incredibly messy and seemingly impossible to untangle. All Jessie could hope for was that Valentine was having more success in her interviews.

CHAPTER SEVEN

Detective Susannah Valentine felt like punching someone.

Things had started off okay before going south. The co-pilot, Ned Waturi, was a pleasant but bland fellow with a soft face and a formidable belly. Unfortunately, he didn't leave the cockpit but once during the flight, to confirm that one of their passengers was dead. Anna De Luca, the junior flight attendant, was a little more helpful.

She mentioned that she and the other attendant kept digital logs of when they checked off specific flight tasks, which they could provide. But for now, she gave a general tick-tock of events on the plane: when the partying started (immediately upon boarding), when people started stripping (about forty-five minutes into the flight), who was serving drinks (everyone, to themselves and each other, all the time), and what happened after Morse was discovered dead (lots of crying, lots of drug stashing, and the immediate cessation of festivities). But she claimed that she'd been so harried that smaller details escaped her attention. Susannah wasn't certain she bought that last bit, but let the girl go for the time being.

The unpleasantness factor increased dramatically when she spoke to the Wards. Lucy, a lean, athletic woman with ripped arms, was nice enough, but she was overtly evasive. Susannah couldn't tell why. Was it because she didn't want to admit to all the drugs she'd consumed or out of some sense of guilt that she hadn't even noticed that her longtime friend was dead while she was six feet away, doing tequila shots? The harder Susannah pressed, the more she shut down.

Dr. Glenn Ward was even more frustrating. A short, bespectacled man with a pale complexion and a sloppy comb-over that left black, cobweb-like strands of hair on his scalp, he was obviously still a little buzzed, which didn't help.

"You, Lucy and Eddie were friends since college?" she confirmed to start off.

"Since freshman year," he told her, before adding snarkily, "right after our first threesome."

"Is that true?" she asked.

"Of course not," he scoffed. "Eddie once described Lucy as cute, like a poodle. He wasn't into her. I never told her that. I didn't think she'd like it."

"You're probably right," she agreed.

"I bet he would have gone for you though," Ward said, suddenly salacious. "In fact, with the way you look, I bet everyone goes for you."

Susannah stared at him in disgusted disbelief.

"Dr. Ward, are you really hitting on me right now, with your wife on the other side of that door and me questioning you about the death of your longtime friend and patient?"

His lascivious grin faded.

"I guess I'm still a little drunk," he said. "Still, you don't have to be such a bitch about it."

And just like that, the interview turned sour. His fuzzy mental state, combined with his general arrogance, embarrassment at being called out, and irritation at being questioned at all, made him petulant. He seemed intent on turning every question she had back on her, as if she was the one who ought to be feeling self-conscious.

"How did you verify his death?" she asked.

"Using my doctor skills," he spat, "You know—the ones that I got at doctor school."

"Do you recall the time you confirmed it?" she pressed, ignoring his sarcasm.

"No, I was a little busy processing the loss of one my oldest friends. I didn't think to check my watch."

She exhaled slowly to allow the exasperation to pass.

"You were his personal physician, correct?"

"Yes. I'm a concierge physician. I find getting direct payments from my patients less complicated than the whole insurance thing. How do you get paid, Detective—in shooting range coupons?"

Susannah smiled mildly, as if humoring a grouchy child.

"As his physician, are you aware of any pre-existing conditions that might have put him at risk for something like this?"

"At risk of what exactly—dying on a private jet returning from his fiftieth birthday bash? No, I'm not aware of anything that pre-disposed him to that outcome. Beyond that, HIPAA regulations prevent me from having a gab session about my patient's medical history. Anything else, Suzy?"

Susannah was tempted to inform him that information could be disclosed to law enforcement when there was suspicion that the death might be the result of criminal conduct. But doing that would reveal that they suspected foul play, and she and Jessie Hunt had agreed not to do that at this point. So she bit her tongue.

"That will be all for now."

She thought things couldn't get worse than that. But Gareth Thacker proved her wrong. The man made Glenn Ward seem like a fuzzy bunny. Because all the other offices were in use, his interview was held in a storage room just off the hangar.

He settled into the folding chair she'd put out for him and spread his legs wide, a leer on his face. She sat down opposite him, pretending not to notice. Before speaking, she looked at him closely for the first time.

There'd been lots of talk in her other interviews about his outlandish behavior but this was the first chance she'd had to observe him up close. She guessed that he was about forty. Physically, he was a mess. His longish blond hair shot in every direction. Several days' worth of stubble covered his double chin. His blotchy face was flushed and his eyes were bloodshot. She could smell the alcohol and pot wafting off him more than with anyone else.

Beyond that, he was disheveled. His shirt, a loud Hawaiian number, was misbuttoned and his copious chest hair was poking out everywhere. He wore black leather pants that were way too tight for his ample waist. In fact, he'd unbuttoned them and the zipper was half open. He had on pink slippers, the only part of his outfit she actually liked.

"So I hear you made the most of the weekend," she began, hoping to win him over before getting to the tough stuff.

"I make the most of every weekend, baby," he told her. "This was one of the best until the last couple of hours or so."

"You sound really broken up about your friend's death," she noted.

"We weren't really friends, sweet cheeks," he said. "More like friendly acquaintances that proved useful to each other. He only invited me to his big bash because he was afraid I was about to jump to another label. He was wooing me."

"Was he successful?" Susannah asked, doing her best to ignore his crass nicknames.

"I hadn't decided. But I gotta tell you, it's not looking too good now. Once word gets out about Eddie, you can count on an exodus of talent. I doubt any artist not under contract will stick around. It's not like his partner, little Joey Baldwin over there, is good at the relationship thing. He's better with numbers. Not that he'll care. After that Middle Eastern outfit gave them a cash infusion, he's rolling in it.

He'd probably be happy to re-issue the label's catalogue in greatest hits compilations and watch the cash flow in."

"So you don't think he's upset about Eddie's death?" she asked, wondering if getting such a massive bailout might have a deleterious effect on Baldwin's mindset. Was there any chance that the guy might want to get out of the rat race badly enough that he'd be willing to eliminate the one major obstacle to that: his partner?

"I didn't say that, miss lady lumps," he countered, popping each word grotesquely. "I'm sure he's broken up over it. I'm just saying that from a cash money perspective, he's probably good either way. And now he doesn't have to deal with Eddie's…volatility."

"What does that mean?"

Thacker smiled wryly.

"Just that Edward Morse could be a little combative from time to time. And I say that as someone with a well-earned reputation for being a top-tier asshole."

Susannah could tell he wasn't going to share more gossip than that and decided to switch topics, hoping to catch him off guard.

"What do you remember about him on the flight? Did you notice that he seemed ill at any point?"

"Listen hot stuff, I'm going to be straight with you" he said conspiratorially, "I don't remember much about the flight. I confess that I imbibed a few adult beverages and consumed some other mind-altering substances."

"Do you really expect me to believe that you don't remember anything?" she asked flat out.

"It's true," he insisted with a sneering grin. "Other than providing my fellow passengers with a free striptease, most of my time up there is hazy. Having said that, if you had been on that plane, I'm pretty sure my recollection would be clearer. Speaking of which, how much would it cost me to get a little private lap dance right now, maybe with some extras? I've got five hundred in my wallet. Hell, if you've got a halfway decent singing voice, I could get you a recording contract, though probably not at Eddie Records anymore."

That was about the time that Susannah got the urge to throw that punch. Instead she stood up and, not wanting to give Thacker the satisfaction of knowing he'd gotten to her, gestured elaborately for him to leave the storage room.

"You can go back to the office you were in, Mr. Thacker," she said as professionally as she could. "We'll let you know where things go from here momentarily."

He stood up and started to shuffle out, obviously disappointed that he hadn't gotten her worked up.

"You sure you don't want to take me up on that offer?" he whispered dramatically as he ambled past.

"Not unless you want to get arrested for solicitation," she whispered back with equal theatricality.

As she watched him make his way back to the office, she tried to paint a picture in her mind. It was clear that everyone she'd spoken to, with the exception of the co-pilot, was hiding something. The Wards, despite their shared friendship with Morse, didn't seem as broken up as she would have expected. And though he pretended to be an open book, it was clear that Gareth Thacker was using his outsized personality and claims of drug-induced amnesia to mask something. Even Anna the flight attendant seemed to be holding back. But hiding something didn't automatically equate to murder. And she hadn't found anything yet that tied one of them to that.

She saw Jessie Hunt standing at the far end of the hangar, waving at her. She waved back and headed over. As she did, she straightened her back and adopted her most confident stride. The last thing she needed was for the legendary, intimidating profiler to question whether she was up to this task.

It was strange to think that Hunt was only two years older than her. The woman seemed so much more mature and accomplished, likely because she was. And now, after weeks of trying to prove her mettle to the profiler from afar and worrying that she was failing miserably, she was finally getting the chance to work with her and show her that she deserved to be here, on the HSS team, in her company.

Hunt had a look of grim determination her face. Susannah didn't know her well enough to determine if that meant she'd made some kind of breakthrough in her interviews or that she'd come up empty too. Either way, she was about to find out.

CHAPTER EIGHT

Hannah Dorsey stood at the bank of elevators in the lobby, waiting to see which one would take her to her moment of reckoning.

Once one arrived and she stepped inside, it would take her up to the office of Dr. Janice Lemmon, the highly regarded psychiatrist and former criminal profiling consultant who happened to be her therapist. When their 2 p.m. session started, Hannah intended to finally tell Lemmon what she'd originally planned to say two weeks ago and then again last week, but never did: that she was a cold-blooded murderer, and worse, that she liked it.

It happened a little over a month ago, at an isolated log cabin in the picturesque mountain town of Wildpines. She, Jessie, and Ryan had gone there to evade the elderly serial killer called the Night Hunter. Somehow, he still found them and almost killed them all before they managed to outwit him.

But once he was incapacitated, sitting on the floor in handcuffs, still taunting them, she shot him, shutting him up forever. At the time she'd told herself that she had no choice, that as long as he was still alive, the man would find a way to come after them or get someone to do it on his behalf. That might have been true. But looking back now, that wasn't why she had done it.

She had killed him because she could, because she was curious to learn how it would make her feel, and because she was nearly certain that she wouldn't face consequences for gunning down a man who had murdered hundreds of people over the years.

She was right on that last point. Jessie, Ryan, and an older woman who'd been held hostage by the Night Hunter all covered for her that night, letting the investigating cops believe that she'd acted in self-defense. And she'd satisfied her curiosity too. It turned out that killing another human being, or at least this one, gave her a thrill that she'd never felt before.

For as long as she could remember, even before her adoptive parents were slaughtered by her birth father—the one she shared with Jessie—she'd been trying to feel emotions like other people did. For her, they were all muted, as if the volume was turned way down on her entire limbic system. Only in the last year had she discovered that the

35

most effective way to generate any kind of real feelings was to put herself in heightened, sometimes dangerous situations.

That meant confronting a drug dealer in a public park. It meant using herself as bait to help her sister bust an underage sexual slavery ring. It also meant sneaking into the house of a convicted pedophile to find proof that he'd abducted a girl, as well as falsely accusing multiple scumbags of assaulting her. All of those acts had made her heart beat harder and her blood pump faster. But they weren't enough.

Killing someone seemed like the next logical step. And when the opportunity presented itself in the form of a captured serial killer, she had taken it without a second thought. And it was everything she'd hoped for. The rush of adrenaline that shot through her entire body made all her extremities tingle at the same time. A wave of euphoria cascaded from the back of her brain to the front and then back again. She'd never had sex or shot heroin but imagined this was what it must be like to do both at the same time.

And then it started to fade. The sweet taste lingered for a few minutes, but by the time the police arrived at the cabin it had disappeared completely, replaced by much less powerful feelings: apprehension about the consequences of her actions, guilt that she'd put her sister in this position, and a mild sensation that she later identified as something close to shame.

But they all paled in comparison to the initial ecstasy she got when she saw the life drain out of the Night Hunter. And in the weeks since, she'd found herself longing to recapture that feeling, missing it like a phantom limb.

She knew that wanting to get back to that place inside her was wrong, that the desire could send her down a horrible road. Killing a man who'd threatened her family's lives was one thing. After all, Jessie had killed people. Ryan had killed people. But neither had done it unless the act saved their own life or someone else's in that moment.

Hannah was less interested in that distinction and it scared her. Even before she first began to comprehend the darkness in her, she already had a lot of the "potential threat to society" boxes checked on her personality profile. For example, Xander Thurman, the father she shared with Jessie, had been a serial killer. In addition, Thurman's protégé, Bolton Crutchfield, had kidnapped her in the hopes of molding her into a murderer too. She seemed almost destined to follow a similar path.

If she wanted to avoid ending up like her father, Crutchfield, or the other killers that her sister tracked down for a living, she needed help.

And according to Jessie, no one was better equipped to do that than Janice Lemmon, the therapist she insisted had helped her through her own many traumas. So, as Hannah had so often in recent weeks, she again stood in the lobby of the doctor's office building, waiting for that elevator to take her up to face her demons and, hopefully, find salvation.

She stared at herself in the reflection of the gleaming elevator doors. No one would guess that the person looking back at her had the potential for such darkness. Any passerby would merely see a pretty girl who looked a half decade older than her seventeen years.

She was almost as tall as her sister and had the same green eyes, but she was skinnier and had blonde hair instead of brown. She knew that she made heads turn when she walked, though she hadn't really used that asset for anything other than trapping predators.

Maybe I should work on that bad habit once I resolve all the "I enjoyed killing someone" issues.

The elevators doors she'd been staring at opened. It was empty. A man in a business suit brushed past her, stepped inside, and pushed a button. She wanted to join him but found that her feet wouldn't move. The doors started to close. The man in the suit put his hand out to stop it and looked at her, perplexed.

"Are you getting in?" he asked.

Was she? If she did, in less than five minutes, she could be unloading the burden she'd been carrying all these weeks. Then it would be someone else's problem to solve. She knew that Jessie desperately wanted her to come clean and she feared that if she waited much longer, her sister might tell Lemmon herself. She knew getting in the elevator was the healthy, smart thing to do. And yet her feet still wouldn't move.

"No," she said to the man, "you go ahead."

He shrugged and removed his hand. The doors closed. Hannah turned around, walked back outside, and looked at her surroundings. Dr. Lemmon's office was in a downtown building, just down the block from a park that overlooked the city. She headed that way.

She wanted to go home but knew that Ryan was there, recuperating from his ankle thing, and that he'd wonder why she was back so early. She wasn't ready to answer that question. She didn't feel like telling him that she worried that if she told Dr. Lemmon the truth, the woman might call the cops on her then and there, doctor-patient confidentiality be damned. Jessie had assured her that wouldn't happen but as Hannah had learned the hard way, Jessie wasn't infallible.

37

When she got to the park, she walked to an unoccupied bench under a large tree. The park was filled with homeless people. One of them, a man who looked sixty but could have easily been forty, was sitting at the base of the tree, using the trunk as a backrest. He opened his eyes lazily as she approached.

Some small part of her hoped that he'd say something, or try to approach her, so that she could get into a confrontation. The possibility of danger would at least invigorate her, and replace the humiliation she felt at having chickened out once again. But apparently not viewing her as a threat, the man closed his eyes again.

With the moment gone, she chastised herself silently, remembering that it was the very desire to seek out conflict in order to feel alive that had her in this predicament in the first place. Even while trying to get a handle on her freakiness, she couldn't help being a freak. The last thing she needed was to give Dr. Janice Lemmon a front row seat to her sickness.

There was no way she could tell her the truth.

CHAPTER NINE

Jessie was ready to give up.

After spending twenty minutes with Valentine in Jonah Navasky's office, trying to piece together a timeline of events, she was at her wit's end. They were able to recreate most of the wild weekend, including the equally bacchanalian flight to the Bay Area and the time on the island. But from the moment the group boarded the flight back to L.A. until the discovery that Morse was dead, everything was jumbled.

"There has to be some other way to go about this," she said, though she couldn't think of one.

"I say we just go at them harder," Valentine countered. "We know at least some of their stories are sketchy. Maybe if we put the screws to them, someone will crack."

Jessie was about to reply when a pair of loud, angry, female voices echoed through the hangar. She and Valentine darted out of the office to find the source of the sound. It didn't take long. Over near the back offices where the passengers and crew had been kept, Vivien Baldwin and Lucy Ward were screaming at each other. Their respective husbands were trying to hold them back and several uniformed officers stood awkwardly nearby, unsure how to respond. The plane crew stood off to the side, horrified. Gareth Thacker seemed to love what he saw. Patricia Morse was nowhere to be found. Jessie and Valentine hurried across the vast expanse.

"I'm so sick of your damn complaining," Ward shouted. "We get it. You want to leave. But our friend, a guy I've known for over thirty years, is dead. The authorities are doing their best. His body's not even cold yet. Can't you postpone your mani-pedi a few hours to let them finish their investigation, Viv? Or is that too much to ask of you?"

"Oh please," Baldwin shot back. "You know that if you miss one friggin' CrossFit WOD, you'd start to spiral. Not everybody has to carry a tree trunk around on their shoulder to stay centered, Lucy. So don't begrudge me my moment of Zen."

"I don't," Ward countered. "I'm just asking you to have a little decency. Patricia's sitting in that office over there, dealing with the death of the man she loved, trying to figure out how she's going to raise two teenagers on her own, and you can't wait a little longer to get pampered. It's ugly, Viv. Can't you see that?"

Jessie and Valentine finally reached the group.

"Settle down, folks," Valentine said. "This isn't helping anyone."

Vivien Baldwin turned to face them and redirected her vitriol on the detective. Her whole body was shaking, which made both her bottled blonde hair and her fake breasts bounce wildly.

"Maybe if you people were a little better at your jobs, we could get on with our lives. Why the hell are we still here?"

Jessie saw Valentine gearing up to respond in kind and jumped in to short circuit it.

"We understand your frustration," she said, her calm tone masking her disdain for this woman. "And we're doing the best we can to move expeditiously. But this is a police investigation and we won't be rushed."

"But—" Vivien Baldwin started to say before Jessie steamrolled through her.

"Despite a lack of forthrightness from some of you, we know there were copious amounts of drugs on board. As a result, we can't just assume Mr. Morse's death was due to natural causes. If he overdosed, we need to determine that. And getting combative won't make the process go any faster."

Joe Baldwin stepped in front of his wife. Tall and solidly built, he looked like he enjoyed working out as much as Lucy Ward. At forty-four, he was younger than his business partner, and had neatly trimmed blond hair and thin glasses that Jessie suspected might just be for effect.

"We get that," he said irritably. "And we're all upset at Eddie's passing. But the world doesn't stop for us just because it did for him. I have a business to salvage, the very business we shared, and until I can get back to my office, I'm doing it with one hand tied behind my back. Once this breaks in the press, it will have massive repercussions. I need to get ahead of that, not just for me and my wife but for Patricia and her kids. Their future is at stake too. So this needs to wrap up ASAP."

"It will wrap up when we get the answers we need," Valentine said firmly, "and not a moment before."

"We'll see about that," Baldwin replied huffily. "I've been keeping my powder dry until now, but rest assured, there are calls I could make that would short-circuit this whole endeavor. I don't want to go that route but I will if I have to."

Jessie gave him her best, fake "I'm so happy to be here with you" smile and leaned in close to him.

"May I speak to you privately for a moment, Mr. Baldwin?"

He nodded and followed her until she came to a stop thirty feet away from the others.

"I didn't want to say this in front of your friends, sir," she whispered. "I'd hate for you to lose face with them or with your lovely wife. But you should know that our unit has full discretion to run our investigation as we see fit. We are immune from political considerations. So I wouldn't want for you to get too far out on a limb and end up having it break."

He looked like he had a comeback ready but she pressed on before he could give it.

"Why don't you and I make a deal?" she suggested. "We'll do our best to resolve this case in a timely manner and you help us make that happen by keeping the interruptions, complaints, and bickering to a minimum. That way, we both benefit. Sound good? Great."

She returned to the group without waiting for his answer. They were all staring at her, waiting to learn what had gone down.

"Thanks again for your patience, folks," she said to them all. "As I said to Mr. Baldwin, we're working feverishly to dot our i's and cross our t's. We have a little more work to do to get there. So please, return to your respective offices. We'll let you know when we have more to share."

Almost everyone, even Gareth Thacker, shuffled back to the offices without argument. Vivien Baldwin looked at her husband expectantly. But he only nodded and motioned for her to join him in the office where they'd been camped out. Jessie glanced at the far office and saw that Patricia Morse, who had never come out of it, was bent over in her chair, resting her head in her hands.

As Jessie and Valentine headed back to Navasky's office, the detective moved close to her and whispered, "What did you say to Baldwin?"

"I politely told him that his threats wouldn't work and he'd look like an idiot in front of his wife, so he'd be wise to back down."

"Is that true?" Valentine asked. "He doesn't have the juice to cause us trouble?"

"I actually have no idea," Jessie admitted. "He definitely can't shut us down. But can he make our lives difficult? Depends on who he knows and how hard he pushes. That's why I recommend we take a different tack."

"What's that?" Valentine asked as they reached the office.

Jessie closed the door and turned to the partner she hadn't chosen, didn't want, and generally disliked. She knew that the woman who wanted to "put the screws" to people wouldn't like what she had to say, so she tried to be as diplomatic as possible.

"I think we may need to consider letting these folks leave."

"What?" Valentine demanded. "Why?"

Jessie treaded lightly. She needed the detective to be on the same page with her.

"I think part of the problem we're having getting information from these people is that they're all here together," she said. "With their friends around, constantly giving each other glares of warning, everyone's hesitant to spill. But if we release them, then re-interview them elsewhere, where the others aren't hovering nearby, we may be able to put a little more pressure on them, get them to open up a little more."

"But aren't you worried that if we cut them loose, they'll come to the station all lawyered up?"

"Who says we have to have them come to the station?" Jessie asked. "We can talk to them somewhere that they feel more comfortable, when they don't have lawyers around, and are more apt to tell the truth. How about it?"

To her surprise, Valentine shook her head vigorously.

"I think it's a mistake," she said sharply. "If we let them go, that means we're letting a killer go, one who could hop a private jet to a somewhere without an extradition treaty. We can't chance it. I say no."

Jessie sighed. Technically, despite Susannah Valentine's comparative inexperience in HSS, as the detective on the case, she had seniority over a profiling consultant. If she didn't want to let these people go, they weren't going anywhere.

That meant Jessie was stuck here, following an investigative path she didn't believe in, with a cop she was growing to despise.

CHAPTER TEN

She had to get out of there.

Using the "I need some fresh air" excuse, Jessie stepped out of the hangar into the chilly outdoors to gather herself and let her irritation subside. She tried to see it from Valentine's perspective. Since joining HSS, this was her first case as the primary detective. It was understandable that she didn't want to take any risks that might allow a murderer to escape their grasp.

But there were ways to prevent that. They could demand everyone's passports. They could put surveillance teams on all the passengers and crew until they had a chance to re-interview them. They had options.

By going this harsher route, Jessie worried that they'd only make these entitled people dig their heels in more. She was skeptical that they'd learn anything else of value at this location. But Valentine had come to her verdict. Deciding that she needed to move on to something that wasn't out of her hands, Jessie called Jamil to see if he'd had any success learning more about Eddie Morse.

If anyone would have, it would be Jamil Winslow. The young police researcher, who had recently been assigned exclusively to HSS, had a knack for finding evidentiary needles in bureaucratic and technological haystacks. At just twenty-four, he was more prolific than most researchers twice his age.

"HSS research," an unfamiliar female voice said when she called Jamil's office line. "How can I help?"

"I'm sorry," Jessie said, "This is Jessie Hunt. I was trying to reach Jamil Winslow. Did I dial the wrong number?"

"No ma'am. I'm Beth Ryerson. I was just brought on as the unit's junior researcher. This is my first day."

"Oh, well welcome aboard, Beth," Jessie said. "I'm sorry we didn't get to meet when I was there earlier. I texted Jamil with a question a little while back and was hoping that he might have some info for me. Is he available?"

"Yes ma'am," Beth said. "He's at his desk. I'll transfer you."

"Thanks, Beth. And please call me Jessie. I've still got another decade or so before I can handle the ma'am thing."

"Yes ma—," Beth began before correcting herself, "okay Jessie."

A moment later Jamil picked up.

"Hello, Ms. Hunt," he said.

Jessie had long ago given up on getting the unfailingly polite young man to call her by her first name.

"How's it going, Jamil?" she asked before adding, "Are you mad with power now that you're a manager?"

"Not yet, Ms. Hunt," he replied. "But the day's not over."

Jessie couldn't help but chuckle at the kid's increasing willingness to come back at her with quips, a sign that he was getting more comfortable in his role within the unit. Still, she couldn't let him get too cocky.

"Are you on speaker, Jamil?" she asked.

"No."

"Good, then can you tell me—is Beth cute?'

There was a long, uncomfortable pause that she relished.

"That's not appropriate, Ms. Hunt," he said quietly. She could almost hear his cheeks flush.

"Hey, I'm just making conversation, Mr. Manager Man," she said innocently. "Would you rather discuss the case?"

"Very much," he pleaded.

"Okay, then tell me what you've got on this guy."

"I actually *am* going to put you on speaker for this, as Beth has been helping me out," he said. She heard a beep and then he continued. "So, most of Edward Morse's business dealings are public knowledge. He bounced around at a few different record companies before starting his own boutique label, Eddie Records, a decade ago. The label struggled for a few years but then hit it big when he signed the band, Klepto. That led to landing several other similar bands. Morse brought on Joseph Baldwin as his partner around that time and the success continued unabated until late last year, when a Qatari firm invested three billion dollars in the company. That's the same firm that owns the jet he died on."

"None of this sounds overtly suspicious to me yet," Jessie said.

"It's not," Jamil confirmed. "We're still looking at his financials, but so far there are no flashing red lights. Having said that, there's something else."

"There always is," Jessie muttered.

"I'm going to hand it off to Beth at this point," Jamil said, "as she did the legwork on this part."

"Right," Beth said, taking over without a pause. "The interesting thing we discovered was that Morse had a 'Me Too' problem."

44

"Shocking," Jessie said, completely unsurprised. "Go on."

"About a year ago, a former employee posted on social media about a regular pattern of sexual harassment from him: constantly making inappropriate, lewd comments and sometimes more overt advances. She said he even offered her a raise and promotion if she'd 'meet his needs,' which she claims he proceeded to describe in detail."

"How did it all shake out?" Jessie asked.

"He denied everything," Beth answered. "He said that she was a mediocre employee and that when she didn't get the promotion she wanted, she got vindictive and made these false allegations. And since she never formally reported her allegations to HR, but instead just quit, there was no way to verify her claims. She mentioned co-workers who saw the behavior, but no one would come forward on her behalf. So ultimately, he managed to avoid any major consequences. No artists left the label and the Qatari deal still went through."

"Okay," Jessie said. "That's helpful. Can you look through court records to see if there's anything indicating he had any recent settlements? I realize they might be sealed but maybe we can discern some kind of pattern."

"Yes ma—, yes Jessie."

"Great. Let me know if you find anything else. I'm going to get back to it. You've given me an idea. Keep up the good work. I look forward to meeting you soon, Beth."

She hung up and returned to Navasky's office, where Susannah Valentine was staring at the whiteboard where they they'd scribbled names and timelines. She looked frustrated.

"I've got an idea," Jessie said.

"What's that?" Valentine asked, dragging her eyes away from the board.

After sharing what she'd just learned from the researchers, she came to her point.

"If we're going to keep these people here, I think we need to try something new."

"I'm open to new," Valentine said. "What did you have in mind?"

"Let's assume for the moment that the allegations from that former employee are legit," Jessie said. "That would suggest that in addition to being a drug-fueled party animal, Eddie Morse had no compunction about stepping out on his wife. But if that's true, we're not going to get the real story from the grieving widow, Patricia Morse, or from these couples whose lives are intertwined with and dependent on Morse."

"Then who do we get it from?" Valentine asked.

"The person who would have had a front row seat to Eddie's misbehavior, didn't have any sense of obligation to keep his secrets, and doesn't have a family that might blow up if he told the truth: Gareth Thacker."

Valentine thought about it for a moment.

"Okay, that makes sense," she said reluctantly, "But you should know that talking to that guy has been the most unpleasant experience I've had today, and that includes looking at a dead body. Getting Thacker to give us useful, straightforward answers isn't going to be all sunshine and puppies."

"Duly noted," Jessie said. "So we might as well go get him and rip off the Band-Aid."

*

Thacker was smiling.

Jessie suspected he thought this interview would be like his previous one, which Valentine had described to her in repulsive detail. That's why they had changed the location for this new one.

Rather than the storage room, they were in Navasky's office, the one they'd been using as their makeshift headquarters on site. With the whiteboard covered up and any relevant paperwork kept out of sight, it was just another bland room. They altered that a bit by turning up the heat to make it toasty, and then putting a stool in the center of it, one they'd specifically brought in because it was uncomfortably high. That's where Thacker currently sat, a little unsteady but apparently untroubled by being re-interviewed, this time by both of them.

"I figured you two would want to double team me at some point," he quipped.

Jessie noted that he had the slightest slur in his speech, which didn't surprise her. Considering how many substances he was alleged to have consumed on the plane, she was impressed that he was sitting upright. With his electrified blond hair and eyes so red that it looked like he had an infection, he was in rough shape.

"I know you spoke to Detective Valentine about the weekend's events earlier," she said, ignoring his comment. "But we'd like to discuss something else with you. If you can give us honest answers, devoid of lame come-ons, we might be able to get you out of here faster."

46

"What if I don't *want* to get out of here faster?' he countered. "What if I prefer to spend the rest of the afternoon here with you lovely ladies?"

"You're welcome to stay at this hangar as long as you like," Jessie told him. "But if you're unhelpful, it will be alone, in a cold office, with just a silent police officer for company, and without your phone. So if you'd like to spend your time in our company, you'll need to hold our interest by being helpful. Are you capable of that, Mr. Thacker?"

"Fire away," he replied enthusiastically.

"Was Eddie Morse cheating on his wife?" Jessie asked flatly.

"Whoa," Thacker said, leaning back on the stool and almost losing his balance. "When I said fire away, I didn't expect you to come at me with both barrels."

"Please answer the question," she repeated.

"What does Eddie's fidelity have to do with him overdosing on a plane above the Pacific Ocean?"

"It's our obligation to follow up on all leads, even if they don't initially seem relevant," Jessie said perfunctorily, before pushing back. "I can't help but notice that you seem to be evading the question, Mr. Thacker. It's as if you've suddenly developed a sense of propriety out of nowhere."

"How dare you!" he exclaimed, faux-angry. "I have no sense of propriety and I demand that you retract such a scurrilous accusation."

"Then prove it," Jessie replied, unmoved by his dramatic flourishes. "Was Eddie cheating?"

"You know, normally, I have a strict 'bros before hoes' philosophy," he said with a nasty glint in his eye, "but for you and your legs, which seem to go on for days, I'll make an exception."

"Waiting," Jessie said, as if he'd just said that he admired her pocket protector. She noticed that to her left, Valentine's body language was much stiffer, as if she was on the verge of cold-cocking him.

"Okay," Thacker said, his sing-songy tone replaced by something approaching seriousness. "Did I ever actually see Eddie physically committing a technical act of biblical adultery? I can't say that I have. But have I seen him in compromising situations on dozens of occasions with multiple women, some less than half his age? The answer to that is: does a seal like water?"

"So that's a yes?" Valentine confirmed, engaging with the guy for the first time.

47

"Most assuredly, Miss February," he cackled. "You won't take offense if I tell you that if you had a poster, I'd pin it up in my bedroom."

"Hey Gareth," Jessie said, redirecting his attention away from Valentine, who she could almost feel vibrating with anger. "I learned something really fascinating a little while ago. Did you know that anything that gets flushed down the toilet on one of these jets stays in a holding tank until it's sucked into a tanker here at the airport? Interesting tidbit: we had the ground crew remove the waste. They have the ability to separate organic material from other items, like let's say, large quantities of drugs, many of which are in capsule form that degrade very slowly."

Thacker's grin disappeared.

"What are you saying exactly?" he wanted to know.

She smiled sweetly at him before continuing with the yarn she was spinning. In fact, no waste had yet been removed from the holding tank and she had no idea how fast capsules degraded.

"Two things, actually," she informed him, beginning with a flat-out lie. "First, I'm telling you that we have a medic on site who's authorized to draw blood from anyone we think may be in an altered state."

He sat quietly, contemplating that barely veiled threat, fully aware that his bloodstream was a cocktail of items on a "just say no" list. As he sweated that, she continued.

"Second, I'm telling you that some of our interviews lead us to believe that Eddie may have died as a result of drugs that were later flushed down the toilet, specifically by you," she said, mixing together what she knew and what she was making up. "Now we can pursue that angle of the investigation, or you can stop with the games and tell us what we want to know."

"How do I know that you won't pursue that angle anyway?" he challenged.

"You don't," she told him. "But I'm going to let you in on a little secret. Personally, I think that theory's a long shot. And to be frank, I'm happy to let you go on your way. Hell, I don't care if you walk out of here and immediately start calling up Eddie's artists to join you at whatever label you plan to jump to. But if you stonewall us, then I can just as easily see an obstruction of justice charge in your immediate future. In that case, you may end up walking out of this hangar in handcuffs."

Thacker hung his head and slumped in the chair. Jessie could feel Valentine's eyes on her and glanced over to see the woman wearing an expression somewhere between awe and jealousy.

"What do you want to know?" Thacker mumbled.

Jessie didn't need to be asked twice.

"In a moment, we're going to have you write down the names of every date, location, and woman you can recall Eddie stepping out with over the last month. But before we get to that, I have another more pressing question."

"Yes?" he asked.

Jessie paused before asking it. This was the most crucial moment in their probe so far. The answer Thacker gave them could change the course of their entire investigation.

"Eddie was clearly a serial adulterer," Jessie noted. "Did his wife know?"

CHAPTER ELEVEN

"Can I get you something to drink?" Jessie asked.

Patricia Morse shook her head, which was still resting in her hands, just as it had been when they last saw her. For some reason, the officer in the office where she sat had allowed her to turn off the lights. Jessie flicked them on.

Now able to get a better look at the woman, it was clear that whatever semblance of self-possession she had earlier was now gone. The enormity of her husband's passing had taken hold. Whether her melancholy was actually due to his loss, the perks that might be at risk with him gone, or the fear that she might be accused of playing a role in his death, she seemed unable to generate the energy to look up.

"Mrs. Morse," Jessie said, hoping to strike the right balance of sympathy and firm professionalism, "when we spoke earlier, you were very helpful about giving us details of your trip and about the other guests. But I wanted to return to something else you mentioned."

Morse still kept her head down. Jessie looked over at Valentine, who shrugged uncomfortably. With little in the way of assistance from the detective on the case, she continued.

"You said there were lots of blowouts among the group, that it was a pretty normal thing. You said that even between you and Eddie, things could get volatile, that the conflict was part of what kept things 'spicy' between you. Do you recall that?"

"Of course I recall it," Morse said sharply, looking up for the first time. "It was only a few hours ago."

"Right," Jessie noted, a little taken aback by the intensity of the woman's reaction but glad that at least she was alert now. "I'm wondering what the source of that volatility was."

"What do you mean?" Morse demanded, her red, tear-stained eyes squinting suspiciously.

"I mean, would you argue about money? I know you have two teenagers. Maybe they were a sticking point? Or was it something else?"

"It was just the usual stuff," Morse told her, sitting up straight. "All couples have arguments. Is it really that big a deal that we did too?"

"No, or course not," Jessie assured her. "My fiancé and I can get testy from time to time. What about you, Detective Valentine?"

Her partner looked surprised at the question, which Jessie found mildly satisfying. It was always nice to remind Susannah Valentine that Ryan was taken. When the detective recovered, she answered simply.

"I'm not involved right now. But I've had arguments in the past, yeah."

Jessie turned her attention back to Morse.

"You see, we get it. I guess we're just trying to get a better handle on your relationship. What kind of guy was Eddie?"

Morse thought about the question for a long second before responding.

"I know he had a complicated reputation in the business," she conceded. "People thought he was a shark, that he would do anything to lock down an artist he wanted for the label. And I admit that he liked to party harder than most. We both did. But at home, he wasn't like that. He was a good husband, a good father."

"How so?" Valentine asked, managing to sound genuinely curious rather than like she was probing for a weakness.

"He almost always showed up for the kids' stuff," Morse said, getting teary as she spoke. "Unless he was out of town on business, he'd always make the soccer games and the dance recitals."

"He sounds great," Jessie said. "And how about you guys? Was that magic spark still there?"

Morse screwed up her face as if confused by the question.

"Well, we were married for nineteen years," she said primly, "so something was working."

"Pretty loyal guy?" Jessie dropped in there casually.

"Mm-hmm," Morse muttered.

"I'm glad to hear that," Jessie said. "Of course, and please don't take offense at this, but that's not exactly what we heard from some of the other folks. Is it, Detective Valentine?"

"No," Valentine agreed, seemingly reluctantly. "We kind of got a different picture of Eddie."

"From who?" Morse demanded, her eyes suddenly blazing.

"It wouldn't be appropriate to say," Valentine informed her. "But there was this recurring theme."

"What theme?"

"Just that, well," Valentine said, pretending to be hesitant to bring it up, "we heard that Eddie sometimes liked to—"

Jessie took over, as if she'd grown tired of her partner's seeming reticence to be direct, which she knew was an act.

"We heard that Eddie slept around, Patricia," she said, "like a lot."

"Yeah," Valentine added. "It sounds like he was going at it with everything with two "x" chromosomes. No offense."

Jessie watched the woman closely for any tell on her face that she could read. Next to her, she could feel Valentine doing the same thing. But Morse didn't offer any incriminating reaction. The new widow looked like she wanted to be offended but couldn't muster up the conviction.

"He wasn't perfect," she admitted, vastly understating the situation, at least based on what Gareth Thacker told them. Her voice was so tired and muted that Jessie couldn't draw any firm conclusions about her believability. She pressed harder, hoping to get answers and generate more of a response.

"Did you know about his indiscretions?" Jessie asked. "Did you give him the green light for that kind of thing?"

"Are you kidding me?" Morse half-shouted, finally showing some emotion, before regrouping, "Do you think I'm the kind of person who would just say, 'you go have fun, darling, while I say home and watch the little ones?'"

"You wouldn't be the first," Jessie replied.

"Well, that wasn't me," Morse shot back, the floodgates opening. "Yeah, I knew he was sneaking around. I never saw him do it. But more than once, I smelled perfume on his clothes and found lipstick on his collar. There were phone calls where I could hear a purring voice in the background. I told him I knew what he was doing and he had to stop. He always denied it. And he was very convincing. Whether it was rumors about a singer at the label or an employee who accused him of groping her, he always had an explanation ready. And since I never actually saw anything happen, I allowed myself to buy what he was selling. That is, until Friday."

"What happened on Friday?" Valentine asked, a little too eagerly for Jessie's taste, though Morse didn't seem to notice. She plowed on.

"We were in San Francisco for dinner on Friday. We stayed there the first night before leaving for the island. Everyone was at dinner at this place in North Beach. Eddie said he had to go to the restroom. He was gone for about fifteen minutes, so I texted him. When he didn't reply, I called. He didn't answer so I got worried and went to go look for him."

"Where was he? Jessie asked, though she already had an idea.

52

"In a storage room with the coat check girl. When I opened the door, they were on the floor. He was on top of her with his pants around his ankles. There was no way to smooth talk that. You'd think that in a moment like that, I'd want to take a hanger and strangle him, but weirdly, I was more hurt than angry."

"What did you do?" Valentine asked, this time managing to sound concerned rather than ravenous for incriminating details.

"What could I do?" she said. "I stormed out of there. He caught up to me, still pulling up his pants. He got on his knees and begged me to give him another chance, promised that he was done with all that, starting at that moment."

"Did you believe him?" Jessie wanted to know.

"I didn't know, but I wanted to," Morse said. "He seemed sincere, truly remorseful in a way I'd never seen before. So I chose to believe him. Part of it was the situation. We had this big weekend. It was his fiftieth birthday. I didn't want to blow it all up. Besides, we had two kids together. And I'm ashamed to say it, but I'd gotten used to our lifestyle. So I accepted his apology and tried to move on."

"And did he live up to his promise the rest of the trip?" Jessie pressed delicately.

Morse sighed deeply before responding.

"How the hell do I know?" she finally answered. "He was sweet the rest of the weekend. Even when he was high out of his mind, he was sweet. But I wasn't with him every second of our time on that island. I don't know what he got up to when I was in the lighthouse or bird watching. I made a conscious decision to take him at his word. I guess I'll never know if he lived up to it."

After she finished, Morse seemed to shrink in on herself, as if she'd given all she could and had nothing left in her. She bent over and put her head back in her hands. Jessie and Valentine exchanged a look that indicated that they both felt they'd taken this as far as they could for the time being. They wrapped up quickly from there and returned to Navasky's office.

"What do you think?" Valentine asked as she closed the door.

"Hard to say," Jessie replied. "Certainly, she had motive from a traditional perspective. He cheated and she was clearly furious about it, even if she claimed she was more hurt than mad. On the other hand, she admitted to us what happened when she didn't have to. We might not even know about this coat check girl incident if she hadn't told us. She could have claimed to be clueless about all his indiscretions. If she was the killer, she had to know that telling us about them would put her near

53

the top of the suspect list. Why would she drop a motive in our lap? The fact that she came clean suggests that she still thinks his death was an overdose, that she doesn't realize he was poisoned. I'm inclined to believe her for now. What about you?"

For the second time today, Susannah Valentine stunned her.

"I'd bet money that she did it," she said. "In fact, I'd like to arrest her right now."

CHAPTER TWELVE

Jessie did her best not to physically react.

She wanted to come back hard at Valentine for her "bull in a china shop" mentality and her arrogant certainty about Morse's guilt. If it had been Ryan investigating the case with her, she'd already have done it. But this was her first time working with the detective and getting into an argument that might escalate served no purpose.

If she wanted to avoid a blowup and solve Eddie Morse's murder, she needed to find a way to work with this woman, even if right now she had a strong desire to kick her down the stairs. Plus, as she was reminded when Valentine refused to let the passengers leave, the detective was the one in charge.

"Okay," she said evenly, "why do you think she did it?"

"Several reasons," Valentine said without hesitation. "First of all, she could have told us about the coat check girl as a preemptive measure, knowing it might come out anyway. It's possible that someone saw Eddie chase after her with his pants down or maybe she told someone during the weekend and figured they'd eventually tell us."

"I guess," Jessie conceded. "But no one did."

"She doesn't know that," Valentine countered. "She might have just been covering her backside. But that's not all. If she was capable of pulling off this kind of murder—poisoning her own husband with over a half dozen other people around in a confined space—then she's pretty brazen and pretty clever. I would argue that she's also brazen and clever enough to admit to the coat check girl incident because she knew we'd draw the conclusion you just did: that admitting it would make her a suspect, and why would she ever voluntarily do that unless she was actually innocent?"

Jessie had encountered killers who were just that brazen and clever, so she couldn't dismiss the theory entirely, but it seemed like a stretch to jump straight to it without any underlying evidentiary support. But before she could say that, Valentine added another thought.

"Also, with Eddie now dead instead of engaged in a protracted divorce battle, Patricia can maintain the lifestyle she's become

55

accustomed to. Hell, it might even get cushier, depending on what he left her in his will."

Jessie couldn't deny the strength of that last argument, even if she was less convinced by the earlier ones.

"Those are all good points," she said, trying to be as diplomatic as she could, "but let me ask you something: what if you're wrong?"

"What do you mean?" Valentine asked, her face screwing up in confusion, as if the possibility had never occurred to her.

"What if Patricia Morse didn't do this and we arrest her," Jessie wanted to know. "That has all kinds of consequences. Right now, most of the people out there in that hangar assume Eddie Morse died of an overdose or a heart attack or something. No one thinks a major crime has been committed. But if we bring Morse in and she's not culpable for this, we've tipped off the real killer that we know what they did. They'll have a chance to cover their tracks."

Valentine looked like she wanted to object but Jessie needed to get her point across. It was her most important one. So she kept going.

"However, if we hold off on making any dramatic moves, the killer, assuming it's *not* her, might get overconfident and make a mistake. For that matter, even if it *is* Morse, we might be better off letting her walk for now and seeing what she does next. We lose nothing by being patient. But we could lose a lot by jumping the gun."

Valentine didn't respond at first. She seemed to be wrestling with how to mesh her certitude with Jessie's doubts.

"What about the flight risk issue I mentioned earlier?" she wondered. "Whoever the killer is, they could flee the country."

Now was Jessie's opportunity to bring up what she'd thought to herself earlier but held back on sharing.

"There'd be no reason to flee if they don't think we suspect anything," she pointed out before adding, "Besides, we can have everyone's movements tracked. If one of them shows up at an airport, we can nab them then."

Valentine seemed more convinced now but it was obvious that she didn't want to let go of her pet theory. Jessie tried to ease her away from dying on the Patricia Morse hill.

"Look," she said softly, "this a really challenging situation. None of our suspects, other than the pilots, have a real alibi. Most of them were drunk, high, or both, and don't seem to have a clear recollection of the events on the flight. They were all in close proximity to the victim. Any one of them could have dropped something in Morse's drink without being noticed. At Eddie's insistence, there were no operating cameras on the jet. This is the rare situation where it may be impossible to clear anyone, where we have to maintain our full suspect list right up until the moment we catch the killer. It just seems like cuffing someone before we have any definitive proof of guilt actually handcuffs *us*."

Valentine was about to reply when they both got a call at the same time. Jessie looked at her phone. It was Decker. Valentine held up her phone to show hers was the same.

"Go ahead and pick up," Jessie suggested. "Put it on speaker. He clearly wants to speak to both of us."

Valentine nodded and answered.

"Valentine here," she said. "You're on speaker with me and Jessie."

"Good," Decker said. "I know you're busy but I was hoping to get a progress check."

Jessie sensed immediately that something was wrong. Decker rarely checked in unless there was some kind of issue.

"What's wrong, Captain?" she asked.

They both heard a sigh through the phone before he replied.

"I got a call from Henry Hart, the Chief Deputy District Attorney. Apparently he's golfing buddies with one of the people you're interviewing there, a guy named Joe Baldwin. Whatever Baldwin told him has him riled."

"I thought we collected everyone's cell phones," Valentine said.

"We were idiots," Jessie said, shaking her head. "We should have assumed that a guy like Baldwin would have second one for business. He's probably been on it all afternoon."

"Setting aside your screw-up for the moment," Decker continued, "Chief Deputy DA Hart wants to know—let me make sure I quote him directly, 'why my friend and multiple other contributors to our community's prosperity are being held in an airplane hangar while your team is dithering about, taking their sweet time investigating a drug overdose.' Hart said that unless my team has some bombshell, he wants those people released. So my question to you is: how are things going over there?"

Jessie looked at Valentine, indicating that the detective could take the question.

"Well, Captain," she said carefully. "We may have a bombshell on our hands. It looks like Eddie Morse was poisoned with a massive amount of heroin and all the likely suspects were on that plane with him. But other than the killer, it's possible that no one else knows about the poisoning. They all think he OD'd."

Decker was quiet for a moment. When he responded, his voice was low but clear.

"This is your case," he told them. "And as Hunt can attest, I don't like anyone pushing our unit around. So I'm going to defer to you on this. If you want to keep them all there, that's your call. All I ask is that you tell me how you want to proceed so I can run interference with Hart. What's the plan?"

Jessie looked at Valentine but said nothing. She had already made her case for erring on the side of caution. But the ultimate call wasn't hers. It belonged to the detective who had been with the unit for about a month now. And what she decided could determine whether they ever solved this case. The woman looked torn.

"Well?" Decker pressed.

"We're letting them go for now," Valentine finally said. "But I'd like authorization to put surveillance teams on each suspect for the next twenty-four hours."

"Authorization granted," he replied without hesitation. "I'll get the wheels turning on that. What's your next step?"

Valentine turned to Jessie with her eyebrows raised in curiosity, clearly hoping she might have an answer. She did.

"Our next step is to come at these people hard, really put the screws to them," she said, using Valentine's term as she winked at the detective. "Only this time, we'll come at them when their guards are down. Let's see how they react to that."

CHAPTER THIRTEEN

Andrea "Andy" Robinson was struggling.

After more than a year of incarceration in the Female Forensic In-Patient Psychiatric Unit at the Twin Towers Correctional Facility in downtown L.A., she was having trouble adjusting to her new digs. It wasn't the location. Unlike Twin Towers, the Western Regional Women's Psychiatric Detention Center in the Westwood neighborhood of Los Angeles was a state of the art complex with well-regarded mental health professionals.

Rather, it was adapting to the new rules, the new schedule, the new people, and the new security procedures. She knew there would be an uncomfortable period as she settled in. And as she'd only been here a day, that period was far from over.

But that didn't make it any easier. Last night, while in her comfortable bed, in a secure room where she didn't have to worry about another inmate sneaking in and shivving her, she barely slept at all.

Today, she wandered the expansive recreation room, painted in warm yellows and soft blues, and replete with board games without missing pieces and books without missing pages. As she moved around, trying to understand the patterns of the guards and attendants, she'd briefly panicked, wondering if she'd made a mistake in asking for a transfer.

She shouldn't have worried so much. After all, she'd known that when she offered Jessie Hunt the deal, there would be complications. She was the one who had proposed helping Jessie by providing intelligence on crimes that some of her former fellow inmates were planning. In exchange, Jessie reluctantly agreed to have her moved to a better prison hospital, one where feces weren't smeared on the walls regularly; and when it did happen, the mess was cleaned up more than once a week.

The primary complication was that, along with a more thorough hygiene regimen, this place came with additional layers of security, additional surveillance, and much more attention to the details of patients' comings and goings. It was that last bit that was going to prove challenging.

That was because Andy wasn't trying to break out of the Western Regional Women's Psychiatric Detention Center, or the PDC as the staff and residents called it. She was using it for recruitment. She needed a new group of acolytes to indoctrinate in the ways of the Principles. But gathering them would require some freedom of movement, which she didn't yet have. It would also require time, preparation, and patience, which is why she hadn't spoken to another prisoner since she'd arrived. She needed to be a mystery to these women. She needed them to come to her.

Just as important, she needed to be far away from Twin Towers when her previous set of minions began to put her plans into action. She couldn't be tied to the horrors they would soon be committing at her behest. She needed Jessie to believe she was trying to help stop these monstrous acts, not that she had instigated them. She needed her once and future best friend to feel indebted to her for her assistance. She needed Jessie to start to have faith in her again, to believe that she could be rehabilitated, and eventually allowed to re-enter society.

That was another reason that Andy wanted the transfer to this new place. It was imperative that a fresh group of respected medical professionals, ones whose judgment Jessie wouldn't question, give her a clean bill of mental health. If she could convince the doctors, therapists, and security personnel here that she had turned over a new leaf, that she was making progress, they would invariably pass that information along to Jessie. Winning her friend back over was going to be a laborious process, but Andy was up to it. She was willing to put in the work.

What gave her such confidence was one simple fact: her motives were sincere. She wasn't planning anything nefarious when it came to Jessie Hunt. She just wanted her friend back, the girl who laughed at her jokes and appreciated that a rich socialite could also be a self-deprecating regular gal. Andy longed to recapture the growing intimacy between them that had been so suddenly, cruelly stripped away.

Admittedly, spiking Jessie's mojito with peanut oil after she had uncovered Andy's crime—that she had murdered her lover's wife and framed an innocent maid for it—didn't scream friendship. Yes, she had used her knowledge of Jessie's allergy to try to kill her. But it was a desperate move in a desperate moment. Everyone makes bad choices under stress.

Hopefully, Jessie would come to see that one mistake doesn't define a person. And as Andy continued to help her "solve" the very murders she was secretly organizing, Jessie would see that redemption was possible. Once that happened, it wasn't a long road to reconciliation.

Eventually Jessie would understand that the two of them should never have been kept apart. Andy would help her see the light in whatever way necessary, even if that meant that those in the way of their imminent reunion—friends, fiancés, sisters—would need to step aside, or be made to do so.

But that was a concern for another time. Right now she needed to figure out how to make a very important call later today, and how to do it without raising alarm bells.

CHAPTER FOURTEEN

Jessie watched as the last of the passengers and crew filed out of the hangar.

Once she was alone in the massive space with Valentine, she asked the question she'd avoided with others around.

"What changed your mind?"

Valentine looked at her, perplexed.

"What do you mean?" she asked.

"You were so gung ho on arresting Patricia Morse," Jessie reminded her. "What made you let her go?"

Valentine paused for several seconds before answering.

"Other than not wanting to put Captain Decker in a tough position?" she asked, before adding. "I started to have doubts too, maybe based in part on what you said."

Jessie nodded but didn't reply. She worried that anything she said might come across as rubbing it in. Valentine quickly continued.

"I still think she could be our killer. But two points you made are unquestionably true: First, we don't have enough to hold her, so there's no point in arresting her yet. And if we did arrest her, we would lose the advantage that comes from having everyone on board that jet think Eddie Morse died of an overdose. At this point, that's more valuable than pressuring his widow."

This was the first time Jessie could recall Susannah Valentine conceding any point to her, much less several. She sensed that the detective was aware of that too because she was deliberately hiding her face behind her lustrous black hair. Though a small part of Jessie liked seeing the woman squirm, she didn't want to actively make things more awkward after the admission, so she moved on.

"I guess our next move is to determine who among the people on the jet has the most to gain from Eddie Morse's death. It'll be challenging but we can have Jamil and Beth Ryerson poke around to try to see what he left Patricia in the will. Beyond that, I think it makes sense to go to his office, see what the records there show. That might also give us more insight into the nature of his business and personal relationship with Joe Baldwin."

"Sounds good," Valentine said.

They started to leave the hangar when Jessie's phone rang. It echoed loudly in the cavernous space. She looked at the caller ID. It was Dr. Janice Lemmon. Glancing at the time, she saw that it was 2:45. Her session with Hannah should still be going on. If she was calling in the middle of it, something was wrong. Jessie picked up immediately.

"Hi," she said, trying not to sound concerned in order to avoid piquing the interest of the detective walking beside her, "Everything okay?"

"Hello Jessie," Lemmon said, her voice betraying nothing. "I can tell from your tone that you're in a work environment so I'll keep this brief. Hannah didn't show up for our 2 p.m. session. As you know, sometimes she switches to a video session at the last minute. She has cancelled a few times in the past, but always tells me in advance. I called and texted her, with no reply, so I wanted to make you aware. I'm not overly concerned but thought you should know what's up. Maybe she'll be more responsive if you reach out."

"Thanks very much," Jessie said casually. "Please let me know if you get any updates."

"I will," Lemmon assured her. "You please do the same."

After hanging up, Jessie turned to Valentine, who had a curious look on her face. Despite her best efforts to hide her apprehension from the detective, apparently some of it had bled through.

"Do you mind if we make a pit stop on the way to Eddie Records?" she asked. "I need to check on something."

"Sure," Valentine said, "Anything wrong?"

"I hope not."

*

By the time they got to her house, Jessie's apprehension had escalated to something approaching dread. Hannah wasn't responding to her calls or texts and she'd somehow managed to turn off the location status on her phone, despite parental controls.

They pulled up in front of the house and got out. As she hurried up the path to the front door, Jessie noticed Valentine hanging back a bit. She wondered if it was because the detective didn't want to insert herself into a family situation or if there was a more uncomfortable reason.

After all, Valentine hadn't been shy about expressing her interest in everything Ryan said and did. There wasn't a joke he told that she didn't laugh at, a story he shared that didn't fascinate her, or an opportunity wasted to touch his forearm or toss her hair back elegantly in his presence. Maybe the idea of doing that in the home he shared with his fiancée was too much even for her.

Ryan opened the door as they approached.

"Anything new?" he asked. He was leaning on the doorframe for support. His ankle was wrapped tight.

"Nothing," Jessie said, stopping at the entryway to wait for her uncertain partner. Even under the circumstances, she couldn't help but poke a little. "Ryan, you remember Detective Valentine, don't you?"

"Good to see you, Susannah," he said, not playing along. He looked as awkward about the situation as Valentine.

Seeing him like that made Jessie wonder just how strongly Valentine had come on to him when she wasn't around. It had to be pretty overt for him to be so ill at ease. For the briefest of seconds, Jessie wondered if he might be acting that way out of guilt, but then dismissed it and chided herself for allowing the thought.

"Hey, Ryan," Valentine replied modestly. "Sorry you guys have to deal with this."

"We're used to it," he said before turning his attention to Jessie. "I know you're dealing with this case. I can drive around Hannah's standard haunts to see if I can find her."

"That's okay," Jessie replied. "I want you to stay off that ankle as much as possible. Besides, it'd just be a wild goose chase. If she doesn't want us to find her, we probably won't. Better you stay here in case she shows up. I just want to check her room to see if there's anything out of the ordinary."

She walked back to Hannah's room and made a cursory search, but found nothing unusual. Just to be sure, she called her again and listened for the sound of her sister's phone ringing somewhere in the house. She heard nothing.

For half a second, she considered handing off the case completely to Valentine so she could focus all her attention on locating Hannah. But that idea was quickly, and angrily, replaced by another one: she wasn't going to do anything about her sister. Instead she would return to work and hope for the best.

The days of her dropping everything any time Hannah dropped off the radar had to end. The Night Hunter was no longer a threat. The girl could move about the city safely. She would be eighteen in a little over a month. She was essentially an adult now, even if she didn't act like it.

It was time accept that there was only so much she could do to help her sister and she'd already done most of it. At this point, the rest was up to Hannah. She had to choose to keep her appointments with Dr. Lemmon. She had to choose to stay in contact with the people who loved her. Jessie and Ryan couldn't live their entire lives on pins and needles, waiting breathlessly for her call. The only person who could really make a difference in Hannah's life right now was Hannah. Jessie walked out the room and closed the door firmly behind her.

Returning back to the front, she found that Ryan and Valentine were engaged in a relatively stilted conversation about the case.

"It doesn't sound fun," Ryan observed. "No way to eliminate suspects definitively. No camera footage available to access. No usable prints. I don't envy you guys."

"Yeah, well, it might have been you in this pickle if you hadn't decided to go into handyman mode," Jessie said, giving him a kiss on the cheek. "Just take it easy, keep that foot elevated, and let me know if my prodigal sister returns, okay?"

"That's it?" he asked, mildly surprised. "No APBs? No roving patrols?"

"Nope," she said, unable to completely hide the exasperation her voice. "We're done with that. She can come to us. But if she does, please let me know."

"You got it," he said. "Don't worry too much, Jessie. It's not like we haven't been through this before. She'll turn up."

Jessie nodded. He was right. This wasn't new and stressing without a credible reason wouldn't help. It might actually make her miss something important with the case.

"And good luck to you guys," Ryan added. "Let me know if you bump into any famous musicians at the Eddie Records offices."

Jessie smiled despite the situation. She appreciated his attempt to lighten the mood. Maybe she'd even try to get him an autograph. That is, assuming Joe Baldwin's Chief Deputy DA friend didn't try to have them thrown out. The thought of that made her smile even wider. She'd like to see him try.

CHAPTER FIFTEEN

Hannah should have known better.

She knew she couldn't stay in the park by Dr. Lemmon's office forever, so she'd headed back home to the mid-Wilshire area. But she couldn't go home too early, as it would raise the suspicions of Ryan, who was home with that ankle injury. He'd want to know why she wasn't at the session with Lemmon, assuming the doctor hadn't already called to share her absence. She could go to Tommy's Coffee, her favorite coffeehouse down the block, but she'd be easy to find there and she wasn't in the mood to be found.

So instead, she had her ride share driver drop her off at a local parkette a few blocks away from the house. It had a small playground for little kids, a cement wall for people who wanted to play handball or do some solo work on their tennis game, a half basketball court that was used just as often by teen skaters, and a few shaded benches.

That's where she had settled in—on a wooden bench under a large tree—before realizing her mistake. With everyone only having a half-day of school today, there were lots of other neighborhood kids her age looking for ways to entertain themselves. Some were smoking under trees on the grassy section near the court. A few were playing basketball. And there were a half-dozen guys skateboarding along the edge of the court. She recognized one of them right away.

She didn't know his name but everything else was familiar from their one previous meeting. He still had the greasy black hair and acne-covered face. Blockily built, he was her height but about forty pounds heavier. Just as at their last encounter, he had on black jeans with a pocket chain attached. The only difference of note was that, unlike the black Insane Clown Posse t-shirt he wore under his jacket last time, this time the shirt was gray and touted the band Limp Bizkit.

Just two weeks ago, she'd rescued a younger kid in a nearby convenience store from the skater, who'd been trying to pressure him to shoplift a beer for him. She'd challenged the skater and when he'd turned his ire on her, she'd screamed bloody murder, accusing him of trying to grope her. The store clerk had chased him out and that was the end of it—until now.

She hadn't seen him in the interim, didn't even know if he went to her large high school. But at the moment, he was playing a game with his buddies, where they raced from one end of the court to the other on their skateboards, while trying to shove the others so they'd lose their balance and fall down.

He hadn't noticed her yet but Hannah knew that once he did, he'd remember her and she doubted it would be fondly. She'd made quite an impression in the store, first by seemingly arousing his teen boy hormones to distract him from the younger kid, then by freaking him out and sending him running.

Now that he was in an unsupervised area, surrounded by five friends who might quickly turn into a ravenous pack if nudged, she felt at a distinct disadvantage. It was unlikely that anyone would come to her aid if things got ugly, or that they could do much to help her if they tried.

For a few seconds she didn't move, debating how best to handle the situation. Skater Guy was less than fifty feet from her so getting up and hurrying off might draw his attention. Staying where she was surely would. Eventually she decided the best move was to leave slowly and as inconspicuously as possible.

She turned to her right, away from him, put on her sunglasses and pretended to fiddle with her small backpack for a few seconds before standing and walking away from the group in the direction of the small building that housed the restrooms and the groundskeeper's storage room. She was halfway there when she heard him.

"Hey baby, I remember you," he called out and she knew without looking that he was talking to her. "You cost me a beer a while back. I think you owe me."

She continued walking slowly, as if she had no idea his catcall was intended for her. There was no point in heading toward the restrooms. They could easily follow her inside and she'd be trapped in there. The groundskeeper was nowhere in sight, not that he was any match for six unruly teenage boys anyway.

She moved past the playground, which was slightly elevated and filled with woodchips to protect any children who might fall off the play structure. Off to the side was a large, empty stroller that belonged to the one nearby mother, who was pushing her toddler on a swing. That gave her an idea. The teen guys couldn't navigate across the playground surface on their skateboards. To catch up to her, they'd have to stay on the same narrow sidewalk she was currently traversing, between the playground and a metal chain link fence that backed up to a small strip center.

She swung her backpack over her shoulders and waited until Skater Boy was closer. She could hear his board moving fast as he nastily called out, "Ready to make it up to me, baby?"

That's when she grabbed the stroller and yanked it into the path right behind her, ignoring the protestation of the mother. Without looking back, she broke into a sprint. As she reached the end of the fence, she heard a thud and a grunt, followed by multiple other thumps and curses.

Only as she rounded the fence did she look back to see that Skater Guy had collided into the empty stroller and hit the ground, after which two of his buddies had slammed into him and toppled over too. The three remaining guys had hopped off their boards in time to avoid getting taken down and were trying to help their friends up.

"I'm fine!" Skater Boy snarled. "Go after her!"

She lost sight of them as she darted around to the front of the strip center and dashed past the kids' haircut place and the dry cleaner, curling around the side of the latter and back to the chain link fence. She peeked out at the sidewalk she'd just left in time to see all six guys rounding the corner to the front of the strip center.

Once they were out of sight, she leapt up, grabbed the top of the fence and hauled herself over. Then she dropped back down to the sidewalk she'd just come from and lay flat on her stomach. The sidewalk was about three feet lower than the parking lot of the strip center, so that the edge of the lot created a small wall dividing the two sections. It was high enough to obscure her, assuming the guys didn't get too close to it.

Hannah looked to the left to find the mother whose stroller she'd used as an obstacle, walking briskly her way with the child in her arms, her ponytail bouncing aggressively behind her head. She wanted to apologize to the woman, to plead with her not to give her up. But the woman, petite but wiry in her yoga pants and form-fitting sweat top, had a determined look on her face as she came over. Her phone was to her ear. The voices of the guys rounding the corner reverberated through the park.

"Where the hell did she go?" one of them asked the others.

The mom opened her mouth and Hannah winced, aware that she was out of options. But even as she dreaded the conflict to come, some part of her—deep down and seemingly immune to all her efforts to snuff it out—longed for it. As adrenaline raced through her system, she imagined grabbing the guy's skateboard and smashing it into his windpipe. She pictured his friends stepping back in horror as he gasped fruitlessly for breath.

"I don't know where the girl you were terrorizing went," the young mom barked at them. "But I know where you jerks are, which is what I'm going to report to the police right now."

"Come on lady, don't be a bitch," came the reply from the one Hannah knew as Skater Guy.

Looking at the mom, Hannah could tell that she wasn't intimidated.

"I'll be sure to tell them how you spoke to a mother with her child in her arms," she began before pausing briefly, as if coming to some realization. "And after I talk to the authorities, I'll be sure to call your mother, Robbie Fox, and tell her that I saw you here, hanging out with boys who call women bitches. How do you think she'll react to that?"

"Oh man," someone who was obviously Robbie said, "forget that girl. Let's go. Please don't say anything to my mom. We're leaving."

"Whatever, wuss," Skater Guy retorted, but it was clear from his voice that he was facing the other direction and moving away fast. The guys continued skating but the sound of their wheels on the asphalt faded into the distance.

The mom watched them go as she stroked her little boy's head. It was a good forty-five seconds before she finally spoke.

"They're gone now. You can get up."

Hannah crawled to her feet and looked over the wall. The guys were nowhere in sight. She found herself unexpectedly consumed with disappointment and even a little anger at the mom for interfering and preventing the conflict from escalating. She did her best to mask it.

"Thank you," she said, turning back to the woman. "And I'm really sorry about your stroller. I didn't know what else to do."

"Don't worry about it," the woman said. "That was actually pretty quick thinking, not that you should have had to come up with an escape plan at all."

"Well, thanks anyway," Hannah replied.

"What was all that about?" the woman asked as she put the boy in the stroller, "Something about costing him a beer?"

"Oh," Jessie said, deciding how honest to be. "A few weeks ago in a store, I saw him pressuring some kid to steal a beer for him. I told him to leave the kid alone and then he started harassing me. So I called out for help and the store clerk chased him off with a baseball bat. I guess he held a grudge."

The woman nodded, and then looked in the direction where the guys had disappeared.

"Do you live close to here?' she asked.

"A few blocks south," Hannah said.

"I'll tell you what. Why don't I give you a ride home? Who knows where those jerks are now. I'd hate for you to run into them walking home."

"Thank you," Hannah said.

"Not a problem. We have to stick together," she insisted. "What's your name?"

"Hannah."

"Nice to meet you, Hannah, I'm Carrie. This little man is Sam. Now let's get out of here so you can see your family and I can call Robbie's mom. That boy is about to have a very ugly evening."

Hannah got in the car and waited while Carrie put Sam in his car seat and then the stroller in the back. As she waited, Hannah came to a realization that had been circling around her brain for weeks: she was exhausted.

After the murder of the Night Hunter and all the dangerous, subsequent attempts to chase that one moment of euphoria, followed by the lying, the self-delusion and now the running, hiding, and needing to be saved by mother holding a baby, it was just too much. She'd gotten in way over her head and there was no way to get out on her own. She needed help. There were people offering it to her.

It was time to accept it.

CHAPTER SIXTEEN

In Jessie's opinion, Eddie Records was an architectural monstrosity.

The Hollywood building stood near the top of a hill on Vine Street between Yucca Street and Franklin Avenue. It sat just across the street and north of the Capitol Records building and seemed to be competing against it.

The structure was designed to look like a bookshelf with a bunch of album covers lined up next to each other. But with its uneven edges and strange, unjustified gaps, it looked more like an accordion made of multi-colored, corrugated metal.

It was 3:45 and Jessie was just parking the car when her phone buzzed. Once she found a spot on the street, she checked the message. It was from Ryan and read: *Hannah just got home. Dropped off by some mom and her baby. No explanation for that. Said she turned off her phone and then forgot she did it. Refused to discuss why she missed her session. Super fun to be around right now.*

Despite the sympathy she felt for Ryan, the stronger feeling was one of relief. Hannah was okay. And if she was being her usual difficult self, it meant that nothing too terrible had happened to her while she was out. They could work out the particulars later. At least now she could focus on the case without worry gnawing at her every second. She texted Dr. Lemmon with the update and got out of the car.

"All good?" Valentine asked as they walked toward the entrance.

"I know where my sister, who I'm legally responsible for, is. So it could be worse, I guess."

They stepped inside the building and discovered that the album cover theme dominated there too. The walls were a collage of painted album covers interspersed with vinyl records. Unfortunately, the result looked more like alien spaceships against a psychedelic sky: interesting until the inevitable headache kicked in.

The lobby was also littered with multiple pillars, on which rested record players, boom boxes, and even a Walkman. The intended goal was obviously to treat these items as works of art, and in theory it made sense. But in practice, it came across as pretty cheesy.

They approached the reception desk, where a pale, young blonde with pink and blue streaks in her hair and several tattoos on her neck greeted them.

"How may I help you?" she asked pleasantly.

"LAPD," Valentine said, flashing her badge. "We need to speak to Joe Baldwin and the executive team for the label."

The woman nodded as if she got that kind of request from law enforcement every day.

"They're all on level seven," she said, sliding a clipboard toward them. "If you could just sign in and put on these visitor badges before you head up, I'll have our communications lead, Celine Warne, meet you in the foyer."

After signing in and putting on the badges they took the elevator upstairs, where Celine was waiting. Unlike the receptionist, she had no tattoos and her hair was all the same color—brown. She wore stylish glasses, a retro *Annie Hall*-style pantsuit getup and looked to be in her mid-twenties.

"Hello," she said politely. "My name's Celine. I assume you're here in relation to Eddie's recent passing?"

"You've already heard?" Valentine asked.

"Yes," she said gravely. "Mr. Baldwin came by briefly a little while ago to deliver the news to the entire staff. We're all still processing it."

"You say he came by briefly," Jessie repeated. "So he's already left?"

"Yes," Celine told her. "He said he was quite shaken up and planned to spend the rest of the day at home. He said that anyone who didn't have pressing duties today could do the same. Unfortunately, with the press inquiries, contract questions, and a new album from one of our artists dropping tomorrow, most of us need to stick around. That's why I'm here. As long as I am, what can I do to help you?"

Jessie shrugged at her partner, indicating that she should take the lead if she wanted. She clearly wanted.

"I'm Detective Susannah Valentine," she said. "This is Jessie Hunt, a profiler who consults with the department. We're just following up on a few loose ends. We'd like to talk to your head of business affairs."

"Of course," Celine said and led them down a long hallway. Jessie couldn't help but notice that while the ground floor of the building was ridiculously ostentatious, the seventh floor where actual work was done, looked like any other office: drab, with corkboard dividers and fluorescent lighting.

"How was Eddie viewed by the staff?" Jessie asked casually as they rounded a corner.

"Oh, everyone considered him a genius," Celine told her. "His ability to forge personal connections with artists was amazing. He really made them feel like they have a home here."

"Right," Jessie said amiably before pressing a little harder. "But in terms of his personal interaction with employees, especially female ones, I heard that he could be a little more… assertive than some might like."

Celine stopped walking and turned to face her.

"I'm not sure exactly what I'm supposed to say," she said. "The man just died this morning. I feel like it would be inappropriate to be overly critical of him."

"We get that, Celine," Jessie said soothingly. "But we're the police, and in order to close this case, we need to get a fuller picture of the man, not some rose-colored glasses version. So just tell us the truth. It's not like he can do anything about it now."

Celine bit her lip as she considered what to do.

"Okay," she said, pulling them into a small, unoccupied conference room. "I don't want to get too specific, but let's just say that while a lot of us are worried about what will happen with the company going forward, none of us will miss Eddie's personal touches, and I mean that literally. It was like he never heard of Harvey Weinstein. He never met an ass he wouldn't grab or a neck he wouldn't kiss. And when he was high, which was often, it was twice as bad. We'd warn each other around the office to always stay in pairs so he could never get anyone alone."

"Why did people continue to work here?" Valentine asked, baffled.

Celine shrugged.

"Lots of reasons," she said. "For one, I've heard that it's not much better at other labels. And he often bad-mouthed the girls who *did* leave, which made it hard for them to get work elsewhere. Plus, for people who love working with music artists, this is the place to be. You get up close and personal with them and lots of people who started here have parlayed it into great jobs elsewhere. And the company pays better than industry average. Put all of it together and, for a lot of us, it just didn't seem worth the hassle to bail. Better to tough it out until we got an offer somewhere else. Real courageous, I know."

"Don't be too hard on yourself," Jessie said. "It's hard to be a trailblazer for justice when the trail is littered with landmines. We know that his wife was aware of his indiscretions. But do you think she knew about his other behavior?"

"Do I think she knew her husband was sexual harassment personified?" Celine said. "Probably not. But she knew about the lawsuit against him, the one everyone knows he settled. And it's hard to imagine he only did this stuff in the office. She had to have an idea of what was going on."

"Okay, Celine," Jessie said, watching the woman shift uncomfortably from foot to foot and deciding to let her off the hook, "I think we have all we need for now. Why don't we head back out?"

Celine nodded in relief and led them to the office of Marie Nelson, a forty-something woman with tired eyes, who was wearing heavy makeup. She didn't look enthused to have visitors, especially from the LAPD.

"We're following up on Eddie's death," Jessie explained vaguely, not mentioning the potential of foul play.

"What's going to happen to the company now?" Valentine asked bluntly, launching straight in.

Marie didn't seem stunned by the question, which suggested that she'd been wondering the same thing.

"Who knows?' she said, her scratchy voice making Jessie feel itchy. "Technically, it shouldn't be a death knell. We have twenty-seven acts under contract and a deep catalogue to call on. But only five of those acts are consistent money-generators and two of them can renegotiate within the next year. Plus, we have multiple album-to-album deals with some artists. They can walk at any time. And with Eddie gone, a lot of them might. He knew how to massage the talent. Joe was the heavy, the one who got into the nitty-gritty of contracts. No one's going to stick around because of their relationship with him. I think this place can stay in the black for a couple of years and limp along for another half dozen after that. But as a buzzy, talent-magnet label, we probably died right around the time Eddie did."

Jessie appreciated her frank answer. No wonder she was in charge of business affairs. She hoped the woman would be as forthcoming with the next question.

"Joe had to be painfully aware that he was perceived as just a money man," she said. "How do you think that affected his friendship with Eddie?"

She was pursuing the line of questioning that she and Valentine had agreed upon in the car on the way over. They both knew it might lead to some raised eyebrows, but they needed to determine the dynamic between the two men from someone outside their social circle.

Marie stared at her, her fatigued eyes weighed down by her sudden, exponential increase in responsibility. For a moment, Jessie thought she might just refuse to respond out of pure exhaustion. But when she did, she was as direct as before.

"I wouldn't call them friends," she replied raspily. "Maybe they were when Eddie first brought Joe on. But by the end it was more a marriage of convenience. I think Eddie still had affection for Joe, but he was bombed out of his mind half the time so I don't think he noticed that the feeling wasn't reciprocal. Joe seemed to feel that he was the lesser among equals: that no one, especially not Eddie, appreciated what he did. Joe once told me that Eddie should retire from active involvement at the label and just stay on in a figurehead capacity, to attract talent with his name. He thought he could run the place better on his own. I think that was his ultimate plan."

Though her face didn't show it, alarm bells were going off in Jessie's head. Marie Nelson had just described a perfect motive for murder. But before she could diplomatically pursue the topic, Valentine beat her to the punch.

"How badly do you think he wanted to put that plan into action?" the detective asked, failing miserably to mask her curiosity.

Marie's eyebrows rose nearly to her scalp line.

"Are you sure you're investigating an overdose?" she asked.

"We're just following every angle," Valentine answered far too quickly, realizing her mistake.

Jessie decided that, now that the cat was partly out of the bag, she may as well go all the way.

"*Should* we be investigating his death as something other than an overdose?" she wondered.

Marie pondered the question.

"Hard to say," she finally said. "With Eddie dead, Joe is the logical successor to the throne. But according to their contract, Patricia Morse still retains half-ownership of the label. I assume she'd let Joe buy her out. But if not, it could get messy. From where I sit, Eddie being dead isn't a clear win or loss for Baldwin."

Jessie looked over at Valentine to see if she had any other questions. She shook her head.

"Thanks, Marie," Jessie said. "I can honestly tell you what I say to a lot of people but very rarely really mean: you've been very helpful."

They left her office and started back down the hall.

"So I assume there's only one place we should be headed right now," Valentine said leadingly.

"Yep," Jessie agreed. "It's time to talk to the man of the hour. Let's go see how Joe Baldwin is holding up."

CHAPTER SEVENTEEN

Susannah Valentine pretended not to be impressed.

It had been easier back at the record company, where the gaudiness of the building overwhelmed any charm it might otherwise have. But this place was different.

As they got out of Jessie's car and approached the Baldwin home in Marina del Rey, it was hard to keep her jaw from dropping. The entire neighborhood was impressive. Each home was essentially a waterfront mansion whose backyard opened onto the marina. To add to the majesty, it was almost 5 p.m. and the sun was just beginning to crawl toward the western horizon, casting pink and orange streaks across the sky.

The Baldwin place had a casual beach house look, if that beach house had six bedrooms, five baths, and cost over twelve million dollars. As they got to the front door, they could hear loud music playing in the back. Susannah recognized it immediately as one of the yacht rock songs her mom loved to listen to while undergoing chemotherapy. It was "Steal Away" by Robbie Dupree.

"I guess they're not afraid of seeming like a cliché," Jessie said.

Susannah wanted to laugh but held it in. Instead she knocked loudly on the door. When that got no response, she rang the bell. While she waited, Jessie walked around to the side of the house and peered toward the back at something in the distance. A moment later she motioned for Susannah to join her.

"There's a path between their house and the one next door that leads to the dock," she said, pointing. "I don't think that it's part of their property, so there's no reason we can't walk back and see what's what. Okay with you?"

Susannah nodded that it was. If Jessie Hunt thought she was the one who would balk at taking bold action when it came to an investigation, she was woefully mistaken. Taking the lead, she started down the path with the profiler right behind her. As they got farther along the song changed. "This Is It" by Kenny Loggins started up.

Eventually they got to the back and the house gave way to a large, brick-enclosed patio with a gazebo in the center. Just beyond that, lying on two lounge chairs, were Joe and Vivien Baldwin. Several heat lamps protected them from the late afternoon chill. They were sipping champagne and nibbling at a tray filled with cheese and crackers.

Susannah couldn't help but notice that they didn't seem especially broken up over Eddie's loss. In fact, to her eyes, they appeared to be celebrating. Joe in particular looked to be having a rollicking good time, loudly belting out the lyrics. Vivien was positively subdued by comparison, merely tapping her toes and humming along.

"Should we say hi?" she asked Jessie.

"Sure," the profiler replied, "Though I hate to break up the party. Maybe we wait until the song is over. If they happen to say something incriminating in the meantime, so be it."

Susannah liked the idea. Unfortunately, the singing never gave way to conversation and when the song came to an end, they decided to make their presence known. Susannah offered an arm flourish indicating that she didn't mind if Jessie took the lead.

"Hey folks," the profiler called out. "Hope you're recovering well from your traumatic morning."

Both Baldwins turned around, shocked looks on their faces.

"What the hell are you doing on my property?" Joe Baldwin demanded, his face turning red.

"I'm not entirely certain this path is *yours*, Mr. Baldwin," she said. "But that's neither here nor there. We stopped by your office to chat there. But they told us you were home, grieving, so we thought we'd do a wellness check. It looks like you've rebounded nicely."

Baldwin seemed about to object. Just then, as if to reinforce Jessie's point, Leo Sayer's "You Make Me Feel Like Dancing" began to play. He scowled, though his usually outspoken wife appeared slightly chastened by the inconsistency between the recent tragedy and their current response to it.

"What do you want?" Baldwin demanded.

Susannah didn't like the man's belligerence and, deciding it was time to change the dynamic a little, took over.

"We're terribly sorry to interrupt your…what would you call this— a memorial service?" she said bitingly. "But we were hoping to put the finishing touches on our investigation. You don't mind if we ask a few final questions, do you?"

Baldwin stood up. He was wearing sweatpants and a USC sweatshirt. He continued to glare at them, showing no sign that he understood how inappropriate his behavior seemed.

"Not if you don't mind me suing you for harassment. I already made one call that got us out of that hangar. What do you think will happen to you if I make another call?"

Susannah was about to respond but Jessie beat her to the punch.

"I think that your sugar daddy's going to get tired of taking your calls if you bother him too much," she said calmly over Leo's falsetto. "And I think he'll resent you putting him in an awkward position when he finds out that the guy he's been doing favors for was partying the afternoon away just hours after his friend and business partner died tragically. It's almost enough to make two law enforcement officials like ourselves wonder if we should do a deeper dive, just to make sure Eddie's death was really an overdose. What do you think, Detective Valentine?"

"I think that makes a lot of sense, Ms. Hunt," she replied, happily playing along. "After all, based on what we learned at your office, Mr. Baldwin, it sounds like you were angling to push Eddie out of the company. How convenient that he up and dies on a private jet, just feet away from you?"

Baldwin was momentarily stunned. Susannah stole a glance at Jessie to see how she had reacted to the question but the profiler's face was noncommittal. When Baldwin recovered, his voice was as hard as ever but Susannah saw apprehension in his eyes.

"What exactly are you alleging?" he wanted to know.

"We're not alleging anything, Mr. Baldwin," she told him. "We're just asking questions, following leads, you know, police stuff. But I'm sure your good buddy, Chief Deputy DA Henry Hart would be interested to hear what we learn, don't you?"

"What do you want?' he asked, his shoulders sagging a little. For the first time since their arrival, he seemed to be relenting a little.

"What we'd like," Jessie said, "is to get a better sense of where things stood between you and Eddie. Convince us why we shouldn't be suspicious of you, in light of the sudden shift in control at the record company."

Baldwin looked at the two of them and then over at his wife, who had yet to speak and hadn't even gotten up from her lounge chair. In fact, throughout the previous exchange, she'd sat quietly, sipping her drink. Susannah thought she looked tipsy.

Baldwin pulled out his phone and turned off the music right as Leo's voice started to make some nearby seagulls fly away. He sat back down on his lounge chair and motioned for them to come over. They approached the brick enclosure but didn't come onto the patio.

"It's not as simple as you make it sound," he said, slumping back in the chair. "Yes, technically Eddie's death leaves me in control of the company. But what do I control exactly? A label known for its artist relationships, and the person most associated with cultivating those relationships was Eddie. Now that he's gone, it's only a matter of time before there's a talent exodus."

"You can't hold on to them?" Jessie asked.

"Some, sure," he allowed. "We have a bunch of artists under contract. But our biggest breadwinners have out clauses. And it's going to be hard to replace them if they leave. Who's going to sign with us if the man with the magic aura is gone? We'll have to entice them with big dollar offers, which kind of defeats the purpose of signing them. We're trying to make money, not lose it."

"So what happens then?" Susannah asked.

"I'm guessing that even with our recent influx of resources, we'll have to sell off chunks of the back catalogue in a few years, just to stay afloat. But that's just a short-term fix and I'm not even sure it's worth it. It'd be like bailing water on the Titanic. You want a reason not to consider me a suspect?"

"Sure, if you have one," Susannah shot back.

"How about the fact that Eddie's death likely put an end to the company I poured my heart into for most of the last decade? To continue the Titanic metaphor, we've hit the iceberg. It's just a matter of time before we sink. And when we do, the stink of the company's collapse will stick to me, because I'll be the name at the top of the executive list. You think I want that?"

"I guess three billion dollars doesn't go as far as it used to," Jessie noted drolly.

"You'd be surprised," Baldwin replied.

"And that doesn't even account for Patricia," Vivien Baldwin slurred, speaking for the first time. Susannah's suspicions had been right. The woman was drunk.

"What do you mean?" Susannah asked.

Vivien took another big sip before answering.

"Just that she'll probably have something to say in how this all plays out. Now that Eddie's dead, she does own a big share of the company outright."

"You think she'll want to have input in how the label is run?" Jessie asked. Susannah saw her take note of Vivien's inebriated state without commenting on it.

"I doubt it," Vivien said. "She never showed much interest in the details of the label. But she could complicate things for Joe if she wanted to—refuse to let him buy her out unless he sweetened the offer. I wouldn't blame her."

"Why not?" Susannah asked. "Isn't that taking money out of your pocket?"

"We'll be fine whatever happens," Vivien said with a dismissive wave. "I didn't want to admit it back in the hangar but Lucy Ward was right. In one moment, Patricia became a single mother to two teenage kids, with no regular source of income. Even though they're swimming in money, she's still going to want as much financial security as possible going forward. She might push hard."

"Is that something you would oppose?" Jessie asked, turning her attention back to Joe.

"Ultimately, probably not," he answered. "I know you were being sarcastic earlier but Eddie and I really were good friends. Sometimes we got a little competitive—okay maybe a *lot* competitive. But I've known the guy for close to a decade. We built that place together with sweat and endless hours of work. We were tight. But I could see how it might not look like that from the outside."

"If you were so close, then how do you explain the celebration we just saw?" Jessie asked pointedly.

He shook his head vehemently.

"We weren't celebrating," he said. "We're drowning our sorrows the way Eddie would have wanted—with good champagne and cheesy music."

"What about you," Susannah asked Vivien. "Do you have a lot of sorrows to drown too? Were you and Eddie close?"

Vivien finished off her current glass and poured another before replying.

"Not as close as he and Joe were, but I liked him, sure," she said. "The truth is that we were mostly friendly because he was my husband's business partner. It would have been weird not to make an effort. Same with Patricia—we didn't have a lot in common but we were pleasant to each other. Sometimes we got extra congenial, but that was usually when chemicals were involved. They tended to make everyone get along."

"How well did people get along?" Jessie asked.

Vivien frowned.

"It's not like we were having orgies or anything," she replied tartly. "We just let our guard down a little."

"I wouldn't have minded an occasional orgy," Joe said.

"Don't be gross," Vivien clapped back.

"Sorry, babe. I guess the champagne is having the intended effect," he said before turning to Susannah and Jessie. "Anyway, if you're really concerned about improprieties, maybe you should look into the $10,000 in company funds that went missing just after we left the island."

"What are you talking about?" Susannah pressed.

"Yeah," he said huffily, "when I went by the office earlier, one of the accountants showed me a check signed by him made out to 'cash.' He pulled the funds out this morning, from a bank in Richmond, near where we disembarked after returning from the island. I'm assuming he intended to replace it once he got back, but obviously he never got the chance. If you're looking for something fishy, maybe check into that."

"What do you think he would have used that money for?" Jessie asked.

"Hard to say," he replied. "Maybe it was for tips for the flight crew. Maybe it was for the drugs we had on the way back. Or maybe it was for something nefarious."

When Jessie looked over at her, Susannah knew exactly what she was thinking: they had a new lead, one that would be taking them north.

CHAPTER EIGHTEEN

Jessie had Jamil on speaker phone the moment they got back in the car.

"If you're calling about Eddie Morse's will," he said after answering, "I've got bad news. It's going to be hard to get that information in a timely manner without the assistance of his lawyers. And right now, his lawyers aren't interested in assisting."

"I need you to put that on the back burner for a while," she said. "We have a new assignment for you."

"Should I loop Beth in too?' he asked without sounding even mildly put out at the change in tasks.

"Sure. We'll take all the help we can get."

Once they were all on the line, she continued.

"Here's our ultimate goal. We need to be on Eastern Sister Island, which is somewhere near San Francisco, tonight."

"I've never heard of it," Jamil said.

"Not surprising," Jessie told him. "Apparently, it's tiny, just big enough for a lighthouse and a small bed & breakfast. That's where Eddie Morse and his friends stayed over the weekend."

"Why do you have to get there tonight?" Beth asked.

Jessie saw that Susannah Valentine was about to call the new researcher out for the question and shook her head. It was the girl's first day on the job. They needed her help and it would be harder to get it if the detective reamed her out and Beth started to doubt herself.

"Because," Jessie explained calmly, "we think Morse's death may have something to do with a $10,000 check he wrote soon after leaving that island. And once the media learns the details of Eddie's lost weekend, they're going to want to follow up on every part of it. That means the island will be swarmed tomorrow and potential witness testimony could be tainted. We have to get there first. So we need you guys to back-time it for us. What has to happen to get us on that island tonight? We're headed to the airport right now."

"Okay," Jamil said, "give us a couple of minutes to pull something together and we'll call you back."

Once they hung up, Valentine asked her a question that had obviously been eating at her.

"What do *you* think the money was for?" she asked.

Jessie allowed herself a moment to breathe before answering.

"Baldwin's theories could be right," Jessie said. "It could have been as innocuous as getting cash for tips or something sketchier, like buying drugs or paying for some other legally dubious service. You?"

"Those all seem possible," Valentine agreed. "Of course, it could be something as simple as an apology via financial reimbursement to the owners of the bed and breakfast."

"For what?" Jessie wanted to know.

"Maybe for turning their idyllic vacations spot into a drug den?"

"Maybe," Jessie said, not wanting to dismiss the idea. "Either way, we need to find out if it was connected to him ending up dead just a few hours later. And I worry that if we don't get to that island tonight, all hell is going to break loose there and we may not ever find out."

The speculation ended then, as Jamil was calling back. Jessie looked at the clock. He had asked for a couple of minutes. It hadn't even taken him that long.

"What have you got?" she asked.

"You might want to grab a pen to write this down," he told them. "This could get tricky. Let me know when you're ready."

Valentine opened the notes app on her phone.

"Ready," she said.

"Okay," he replied. "Go ahead, Beth."

"Right," the young researcher said, her voice a little shaky. "The bed and breakfast only operates from Thursday through Sunday. But they do allow island tours the rest of the week. The last one of the day starts at 8 p.m. but the boat to get out there leaves the Pablo Point dock at 7:45. The last flight from L.A. to San Francisco that will get you there in time to make the boat departure leaves LAX at 5:50 p.m. and gets into SFO at 6:47. We can book the flight and island tour boat trip for you. Should we use HSS funds for that?"

Jessie, who had more experience with the unit than Valentine, answered immediately.

"No. It'll take too long to get approvals. Even if Decker signs off right away, there are too many bureaucratic hoops to jump through. By the time we get the go-ahead, it'll be too late. I'll give you my credit card number and get reimbursed later."

"All right," Beth replied. "But on such short notice, two round trip flights and the boat tickets are going to come to over $700."

"Don't worry about it," Jessie assured her. "We just need to get there."

"I didn't know profiling paid so well," Valentine muttered under her breath.

Jessie didn't appreciate the dig but wasn't in the mood to explain to her short-term partner how she could afford such an expense. Maybe some other time she'd share the truth with the snarky young detective.

Maybe she'd let her know that some of her financial resources came as a result of a divorce from her wealthy ex-husband, who had tried to murder her. Still more came after her birth father murdered her adoptive parents and she learned they'd left the bulk of their retirement savings and investments to her. And the last bit of her nest egg came when her friend and profiling mentor, Garland Moses, was murdered by the same ex-husband who had tried to kill her. In his will, Moses left her the house that she, Ryan, and Hannah currently lived in.

Even though none of the blood from those horrors was on her hands, to Jessie, it felt like blood money. She wondered what the young detective would say once she knew the story behind it. But now wasn't the time to shame her. They had too much work to do.

"By the way," Jamil said, pulling her out of her thoughts, "Captain Decker wanted you to know that at least so far, the surveillance teams don't show any of the jet's passengers or crew doing anything suspicious, like, as he put it 'booking another jet or driving south to the Mexican border.'"

"Good to know," Jessie noted. "Please update us if that changes."

"Will do," he promised. "But right now, we've got a more pressing issue."

"What's that?"

"Like Beth said, the LAX flight to San Francisco leaves at 5:50 p.m. It's 5:19 right now. Do you really think that you can get to the airport and make it to the gate in time?"

Jessie couldn't help but smile.

"I guess we're about to find out."

CHAPTER NINETEEN

Ryan stewed silently as he re-wrapped his ankle in the bathroom.

In addition to losing a day of work to this ridiculous injury, just when he was almost back to one-hundred percent, now he had to worry about something he'd hoped was no longer an issue: Hannah disappearing.

He'd been foolish to get his hopes up. Yes, the last few weeks had been pretty good, with Hannah meeting her obligations and showing up to places on time. But there was always the fear that it could all fall apart at any second. And now it had.

Once again, she was nowhere to be found and Jessie was worried, putting her sister's well-being ahead of her own as she so often did. He had grown weary of it and if the girl ever showed up, he intended to let her know that.

Just then, he heard the front door open. He knew it had to be Hannah, as Jessie always entered from the garage. Instead of leaping up to confront her, he carefully finished wrapping his ankle. Only when he was done did he hobble out of the bedroom and make his way to the kitchen.

Hannah had gone to her room and closed the door. That was okay. He was hungry and decided to make a bite to eat. She had to come out eventually.

*

Hannah hoped he'd fallen asleep.

She knew it was unrealistic at 5:30 at night, but part of her thought that maybe Ryan had taken some pain meds for his ankle and crashed out on the couch while watching TV. But it wasn't to be.

When she came out of her room to prep some dinner, he was already in the kitchen, limping around, trying to make himself a sandwich. The sight was truly pathetic.

"Why don't you sit down?" she said. "I'll make you something."

"That's okay," he muttered irritably, continuing to fumble with a mayonnaise jar, not even looking at her.

"Don't be ridiculous," she countered. "You look like you could keel over at any second and I don't need Jessie blaming me if you injure yourself again."

He turned around and she was shocked to see that his eyes were blazing.

"You're worried about your sister's reaction *now*?" he demanded incredulously. "After all the crap you've put her through. All the hours—not just today—but over the last year, worrying where you were and if you'd come home alive, in a body bag, or at all. After all that, you've suddenly taken an interest in what your sister thinks of you?"

"Whoa," she said, holding her palms up for him to stop. "Where is this coming from? I thought you were the cool, almost step-guardian. I didn't know that you were going to turn into Mr. Authoritarian."

She watched him gulp hard, as if he was trying to swallow whatever he'd been about to say. When he spoke, his voice was calm and cold.

"Hannah, can I be straight with you?"

"I wish you would," she told him though she wasn't sure she really did.

"I get that you've been through a hell of a lot," he said slowly, quietly. "I won't pretend to understand what it's done to you. In less than two years, your adoptive parents were slaughtered by a man you found out later was your real father. You discovered you had a half-sister and she took you in, became your legal guardian. You were kidnapped by a serial killer who tried to mold you into becoming one too. Your life has been in danger multiple times, some due to events out of your hands, some a result of specific, risky choices you made. And then, just last month, you shot a man in cold blood."

She started to respond, but he held up his hand for her to wait.

"Yes," he acknowledged, "the Night Hunter was a terrible person who didn't deserve much mercy. But you killed him when he was no threat to you. Even without that last incident, that's a hell of a lot for one seventeen-year-old to process. Frankly, I'm impressed that you're not in a padded room."

"Thanks," she said sarcastically.

"But," he went on, ignoring her comment, "you seem insistent on hurting the people who are trying to help you the most. You skip sessions with your therapist, the same therapist who helped Jessie work through traumas just as bad as yours. And worse, you seem to almost enjoy hurting your sister. God knows that she's not perfect. But she brought you into her home and reconfigured her entire life to accommodate your needs, basically going from a young woman without personal obligations to a single mother of a teenager almost overnight. And I've never once heard her express second thoughts about that. Yet you seem to be punishing her for something neither of us understands."

"I'm not punishing her," Hannah shot back, feeling something unusual rising in her chest: regret.

"Then why do you repeatedly put yourself in danger?" he pressed. "Why do you disappear for long stretches and seemingly intentionally avoid staying in contact when you know she has legitimate concerns for your welfare. And why, Hannah, have you still not talked to Dr. Lemmon about what happened in that cabin with the Night Hunter?"

She wanted to come back at him hard. But the pain in his eyes was so raw that she couldn't. Besides, everything he said was true. Every question he asked was valid. But as she stood there, she had no good answers for him, at least none that she was willing to speak aloud.

"There's a pizza in the freezer," she finally said, her voice barely above a whisper. "You should just throw that in the oven and wait. The chances of making that ankle worse will go way down the less you're on your feet."

Then she shuffled out of the kitchen without another word. What could she say? How could she make him understand without confessing that she had enjoyed killing a man, that she longed to regain the thrill she'd had in that moment, that every second since had been a battle between desire and the shame that the desire induced.

She couldn't think of any words to get that across, so she chose not to say any at all. She returned to her room and closed the door. Despite everything that she'd been through, she didn't think she'd ever felt quite so alone.

CHAPTER TWENTY

Jessie fought the urge to throw up.

She'd been so happy that they had made it to the boat in time that she hadn't considered what the trip over to the island might be like. It turned out to be choppy, with huge, rolling waves that disappeared under the boat, making her feel like she was on a fast-dropping roller coaster. Each time the hull reached bottom, a big, frothy spray of salt water exploded upward, drenching the flimsy rain slicker she'd been provided. She glanced over at Valentine, who had a big smile on her wet face.

"My dad used to work on a fishing boat," the detective shouted by way of explanation. "This reminds me of home."

Jessie didn't even try to respond. She was worried about what might come out of her mouth instead of words. Just when she thought her insides couldn't handle any more, the fog parted and she saw the island, less than a hundred yards away. It was both beautiful and creepy. The first thing she noticed cutting through the mist was the lighthouse at the far end of the island, which was operating at that very moment, with the bright beacon light warning that they were approaching what was essentially a giant rock in the middle of the bay.

The lighthouse was atop the bed & breakfast, which was comprised of one, multi-tiered Victorian building that probably looked cozy in the day, but under current weather conditions appeared to be a cousin to the infamous *Psycho* house. Jessie wouldn't want to be trapped out here and couldn't help but wonder why the killer hadn't done the deed in this isolated spot rather than on a busy jet. The boat pulled up to the wharf and hit the bumpers hard. That's when Jessie noticed the ladder.

It looked like the kind of ladder used to get out of a pool, only this one was rusty and flimsy looking, with barnacles on the lower part. In addition, to get from the boat to the wharf was a good ten foot climb, with waves smashing around the edges of the boat the whole time.

Once the boat was secured, a crewman pointed a light at the ladder and indicated that they should begin their ascent. Jessie glanced around to see who would go first. In addition to her and Valentine, there were four other passengers who'd come for the tour. They all looked as terrified as she felt.

That is, all except for Valentine, who stepped forward confidently and began hiking herself up. Feeling simultaneously embarrassed and competitive, Jessie followed, reaching for the ladder once the detective's feet were high enough. She moved slowly and carefully, unable to ignore the gap between the boat and the wharf, where she expected that she'd surely be crushed to death if she lost her footing and fell.

Valentine was just getting to the top when Jessie looked back up. She moved quicker, not wanting to appear overcautious. She was two rungs from the top when her right shoe slipped on the wet surface and she felt her body drop. She desperately clung to the side rails, but felt her grip loosen. Then, without warning, two hands grabbed her just below her armpits and yanked her up forcefully. Looking up, she saw Valentine above her, pulling her toward the top, her face contorted with effort.

Seconds later, Jessie was on the wharf, her body shaking with adrenaline. Across from her, bent over with her hands on her knees, Valentine was breathing heavily.

"Thank you," Jessie said.

"Not a problem," the detective grunted, waving a hand dismissively, though she was gasping for breath. "As soon as I can feel my arms again I'll be good to go."

They stepped aside as the other passengers reached the top, all without incident. A woman at the top of the stairs that led from the wharf to the island proper called out to them, waving a lantern. Everyone followed the light, with Jessie and Valentine at the rear.

When they got to the top, the woman, who was apparently their tour guide, motioned for them all to gather around her. In her fifties, she was a skinny, brittle looking woman with a weathered face and long, gray hair that flew everywhere. She didn't seem to care. Jessie was mildly surprised that she hadn't been swept away by the wind.

"My name is Sally Burns," she shouted to be heard over the gusts and crashing waves. "I'm half of the couple that runs this place. The other half, my husband, Barney, is inside the house with some hot beverages for you. Should we head that way?"

Everyone nodded enthusiastically and fell into step after her as she hurriedly made her way past the fog signal building and the water tank. They darted through a large courtyard with a cistern smack dab in the middle of it, to the door of the inn. When the other passengers were far enough away not to hear, Valentine leaned in close to Jessie.

"How are we going to get her away from these people to ask our questions?" she whispered loudly.

"I'm hoping we can have a chat with Barney while Sally is taking the others on the tour," Jessie said, "Maybe when they go to check out the lighthouse or something."

They entered the inn and followed the rest of the group through a small kitchen to a cozy dining room where coffee, tea, and even hot chocolate were available on the table. Standing by the table was a grizzled gentleman, probably a decade older than his wife. He was bald and had a beard that would have made Santa Claus jealous. He had on overalls over a fisherman's sweater. Just like Sally, he had a wide, generous grin.

"Warm yourselves up!" he bellowed happily. "I know that boat ride over is only ten minutes long, but it can take a lot out of you."

Jessie got some tea but noticed that Valentine didn't get anything. She looked agitated and impatient, like she might start questioning the couple now if she could. After five minutes of sipping and chitchat, which Jessie joined in but Valentine pointedly avoided, Sally made an announcement.

"Okay gang. We're going to start our tour on this floor and work our way up, eventually arriving at the lantern room. I'm afraid you'll need to leave your drinks here. Shall we begin?"

Everyone put their cups down and followed her into an adjoining room. Valentine looked knowingly at Jessie and pointed to the ground emphatically, indicating that they should stay where they were.

Once everyone else cleared out, Barney looked at them, mildly perplexed.

"Ladies, unless you're planning to help me clean up, you should probably join the group. Sally's got some quality tales to tell and you're in danger of missing out."

"Actually, Mr. Burns," Valentine said, stepping forward aggressively and pulling out her ID, "I'm Detective Susannah Valentine of the Los Angeles Police Department and this is Jessie Hunt, a profiler we work with. We'd like to have a word with you."

Jessie groaned silently to herself. This wasn't how she'd have approached the interview. Barney Burns looked taken aback and put down the saucers he had begun to collect.

"What's this all about?" he asked in a hushed, concerned tone.

"You had a group stay with you this weekend," Valentine noted, oblivious to his discomfort. "We need any information you have on what the group did while they were here, who from your staff they interacted with, if there were any unusual incidents or altercations, that sort of thing."

Burns was quiet for a moment, as he tried to process what was being asked of him.

"Why?" he finally asked.

"Someone in the group—Edward Morse—died on their flight back to Los Angeles," Valentine said bluntly. "And we believe it was murder. So we need a full account of his comings and goings, as well as of those he was with."

Burns reached out to the table for support. Jessie was about to move to help him but he steadied himself. After a moment he stood up straight again.

"I'm terribly sorry to hear about Mr. Morse," he said slowly. "But I'm confused. Why are you here to investigate a murder that took place elsewhere?"

That response seemed to agitate Valentine more. Jessie feared that this was going to end badly. She wanted to intervene but knew the detective would take offense. The two of them had already had enough tussles that she didn't want to start another one if she could avoid it.

"We're not at liberty to say," Valentine replied sharply. "Suffice to say, there may be a connection. Now if you could please answer my questions."

To her obvious surprise, but not Jessie's, he shook his head.

"Even if was inclined to answer your questions, I couldn't," he said, still politely but with a firmness that was new. "I don't keep track of our guests' comings and goings. Mr. Morse rented out the whole B&B for the weekend so that he and his friends could have some private fun. Other than preparing and serving their meals, attending to their basic needs, and answering any questions they might have, Sally and I stayed out of their hair."

"What did you mean by if you were 'inclined' to answer?" Valentine pressed. She looked about to blow up.

"I mean, Detective Valentine," he replied in a quiet steely voice, "that we are not in the business of violating our guests' confidentiality. Maybe if you were more forthcoming about the connection our little island has to this crime, I would reconsider. But from what you're telling me, it wasn't committed here. And as I didn't notice anything suspicious, I can't imagine what you need from me. If you have a warrant to search the premises, by all means do so. But it seems that you are way out of your jurisdiction, on something of a fishing expedition, so I'm not *inclined* to lend my time or energy to participating in it."

Valentine's face turned a deep shade of red and Jessie saw her hands form into balled-up fists of frustration.

"Maybe we need to get that warrant and shut you down for a few— ," she began, apparently determined to make things worse. Jessie couldn't hold off any longer and jumped in.

"Sorry to interrupt, Detective Valentine," she said, sounding as syrupy sweet as she could, "but I had a thought."

Valentine glared at her but Jessie stared back, keeping her expression amiable even as she bore into the detective's eyes with her own, willing her partner to step back from the ledge she was on. Valentine seemed about to yell at her, but managed to somehow find an internal pause button.

"What's that?" she asked through gritted teeth.

Jessie turned to Barney Burns but before she could ask him anything, Sally popped her head in.

"Everything okay in here?" she asked sweetly. "I noticed that we lost a couple of folks."

Jessie looked at Barney pleadingly. After a moment, he seemed to relent and his frown faded slightly.

"They'll be right along, Sally," he said. "I'm just helping answer a few questions for them."

Sally, seemingly satisfied, disappeared from view. Jessie turned back to Barney, relieved.

"Thank you, Mr. Burns," she said, giving him her best 'respect your elders' smile, "we don't want to make things difficult for you. And we certainly appreciate how dedicated you are to maintaining discretion for your guests. But I was wondering if you'd be comfortable answering something unrelated to them?"

"Like what?" he wanted to know, still guarded but no longer outwardly hostile.

She decided to pursue an angle that Valentine had circled around in her initial questioning but didn't directly address with him.

"Did any of your employees behave strangely, either during the weekend of Mr. Morse's party, or afterward?"

He appeared surprised by the question and she knew immediately that the answer was yes.

"What does that have to do with anything?" he countered, clearly trying to stall while he considered how to answer.

"Mr. Burns," she said, trying to make both her face and her voice soft, "we are trying to solve the murder of a man with a wife and two children. You're right that it didn't happen here. But it's possible that the events of the weekend played a role in his death. We just need your help. It's clear that something is up with one of your employees and what you tell us could really help resolve this. You're not in any trouble here. You're not going to get arrested. The only way that might change is if you deliberately obstruct our investigation. I know that as a man who prides himself on his integrity, you don't have any interest in doing that. So please, I'm asking you, tell us what you know."

Burns's whole body seemed to loosen up after that. Still, he gave Valentine, who had kept silent this whole time, one last glare before returning his attention to Jessie.

"We have two maids, one who works full-time named Rita, and another who works part-time on weekends. Her name is Bella Cammareri. She quit this morning."

Jessie ignored the sudden increase in the speed of her thumping heart and responded as if his answer was only mildly interesting.

"Any idea why?"

"She didn't say," he told her. "But she looked upset. She was wearing sunglasses when she told us, even though we were indoors at the time. I think she'd been crying. She didn't even give two weeks' notice. She just told us the news, apologized, and got on the boat to head back to the mainland."

"What work was Bella responsible for?" Jessie wondered.

"She was Rita's backstop, and would do whatever was required when Rita was overwhelmed. She cleaned the kitchen and bathrooms. She'd make up the suites, whatever was required."

"So she would have had access to the guests' suites when they were out and about?" Valentine asked, careful not to sound too forceful.

"I suppose," Burns answered reluctantly.

"Mr. Burns," Jessie said. "I'm afraid we're going to need Bella's contact information."

He nodded, apparently having expected the request.

"Of course," he said. "But please, be gentle with her. She's had a rough go of it and has somehow managed to maintain her decency. She's the kind of person it's hard to get upset with, even when she quits without any notice. I sincerely doubt she had anything to do with whatever happened to Mr. Morse."

Neither Jessie nor Valentine responded to that. Both had long ago learned that decency could be a mask and that even when it was real, it still wasn't a guarantee against murder. While they waited for Burns to get the maid's info, Valentine whispered to Jessie.

"Sorry I got so riled up before. Thanks for stepping in before things spun out of control."

"Sure," Jessie said, not wanting to linger on that topic and promptly switching to another one. "I guess we know where we're headed next: to visit Bella Cammareri."

"Yeah," Valentine agreed. "And I have to say, I think that medical examiner, Guglia, might have jumped the gun with her conclusion. Maybe it really *was* possible that Morse's flask was poisoned with heroin ahead of time. It sounds like Cammareri could have had access to it."

Jessie nodded in agreement.

"All the more reason to check on the test results she got for the flask."

She pulled out her phone to see if Guglia had sent any updates. But nothing was loading.

"That won't work," Burns said, returning to the room with a piece of paper in his hand. "We don't get a signal out here. You'll have to wait until you get back to shore."

"Great," Valentine muttered. "We're going to lose valuable time. How long until the boat goes back?"

"8:45," he said. "You're stuck here until then. As long as you are, you may as well join the others on the tour."

Jessie saw that Valentine wanted no part of that but she wasn't in the mood for any more edginess between her and Burns, so she jumped at the chance.

"Great idea," she said, grabbing the detective by the arm and pulling her in the direction the others had gone.

Valentine looked irked but Jessie didn't care. She was just as anxious to get an answer to the flask question and to talk to Bella Cammareri as her partner. But they couldn't do anything about it for now, so she was going to check out a lighthouse tower. Besides, she wanted to project an amiable front in order to model good behavior for the impulsive detective. But the truth was that, just like Valentine, she'd be counting the minutes until she could get back to the mainland.

CHAPTER TWENTY ONE

Bella Cammareri didn't live in a great neighborhood.

As Jessie pulled up across the street from the woman's apartment complex, she noticed the guy on the corner, acting as a lookout for another one hiding in the shadows of a nearby alley. Someone approached the lookout and he directed the customer to the other man, who had what he needed. A little farther up the street, a woman in a way-too-short-for-the-weather skirt stood near a streetlight, eyeing cars that eased slowly by.

Jessie turned off the car and was about to get out when Valentine asked the same question she had fifteen minutes earlier.

"Still nothing from the medical examiner?"

Jessie sighed, hoping to expel the frustration she felt. Even after the woman had saved her from falling into the ocean, it was hard not to resent her hard-charging manner, especially when it seemed to cause more problems than it solved. She wondered if she would be as annoyed if Susannah Valentine wasn't also gorgeous and didn't relentlessly flirt with her fiancé. But since she couldn't forget those things, she couldn't honestly answer that.

"Nothing new," she said, checking her phone. "Of course, it's 9:30 and we only asked Jamil to check on it at nine. We should try to be a little patient."

"That's not my strong suit," Valentine said.

Jessie did her best not to make a snarky crack.

"Even so," she replied, "trust me. Jamil Winslow isn't the type to slack when a request has been made of him. The second he has any information on the results of flask test, he'll call. In the meantime, I suggest we focus on Bella Cammareri. I'm sure you've noticed, but this area's a little sketchy. We should stay alert."

Valentine nodded. They got out of the car. As they crossed the street, Jessie could see the San Francisco skyline across the bay. Even though it was less than five miles away from here, it might as well have been a different universe.

They approached the apartment complex, taking note of the knocked out streetlight nearby. Several people glanced in their direction but no one said anything. The exterior gate to the place was still there but useless, dangling pathetically on just its lower hinge. They passed through and proceeded to the front door of the building, where Valentine looked at the tenant directory to get buzzed up.

On a hunch, Jessie grabbed the doorknob and turned. It didn't give but she could tell the lock was loose. She put her shoulder into it and gave the door a solid bump. It popped right open.

"I say we announce ourselves from outside her door," she said, "Less time for her to make a bad decision."

"You think she's gonna try to run?" Valentine asked.

"Whether she's innocent or guilty, that would be a bad idea, so no. But why chance it?"

Valentine's shrug indicated that she was onboard, so they made their way up the narrow stairwell to the third floor. The lighting was intermittent at best and the carpeting on the stairs had a dank, musty smell. Jessie expected to see rats in every darkened corner. When they got to apartment 306, Valentine pulled out her badge so that it was visible directly in front of the peephole. Then she raised her closed hand, about to knock. Jessie held up her own hand at the last second.

"Let's start with the kid gloves for this interview," she suggested. "We can always escalate things from there. But maybe we try honey before we bust out the vinegar?"

Valentine nodded reluctantly and lowered the badge. When she knocked, it was at a firm, but still polite volume. After a few seconds, they heard movement on the other side of the door.

"Who is it?"

"Hi, Ms. Cammareri, my name is Susannah Valentine. I'm a detective with the Los Angeles Police Department. I'm going to hold up my badge and ID so you can see it. The woman with me is Jessie Hunt. She consults for our department. We just spoke to your former employer and he gave us your address. We'd like to ask you a few questions."

"Which former employer?" Bella asked from behind the door.

"Barney Burns," Valentine told her. "Could you please open the door so we can talk a little more privately?"

There was a brief pause, after which Cammareri replied.

"Okay, but please keep your voices down. I have two sleeping children in the back."

"Of course," Valentine promised.

The door opened to reveal a cute but haggard looking young woman. They already knew from a database search that Bella Cammareri was a twenty-six-year-old single mother, originally from

Oakland, who had dropped out of high school during her junior year and had bounced from job to job ever since.

What Jessie hadn't expected was that, even in her bulky sweats, Bella was a tiny thing. She couldn't have been more than five foot two and a hundred pounds. She had black hair and her pixie cut made her look like she might still be a teenager. Her skin was pale and her pretty, hazel eyes were red, likely from a combination of exhaustion and crying. Most notably, the cheekbone just below her left eye was bruised a deep purple.

"Is that the reason you wore sunglasses when you told Sally and Barney you were quitting?" she asked, pointing at the black eye.

Bella nodded slowly, clearly shocked at how much this woman already knew about her.

"I didn't want them asking me questions," she said. "I just wanted to get out. Can you tell me why you're here now?"

"Sure," Jessie assured her, "but can we all sit down first?"

The girl reluctantly led them the short distance to the living room, where the worn couch had been turned into a bed. She sat at edge of it and indicated for the two of them to grab chairs from the nearby breakfast table, which was chipped and had marker stains on it.

"You sleep in here?" Valentine asked.

"Yep," Bella said, pointing to a closed door behind here. "The kids share a bed in there."

"How old are they?" Jessie asked, though she knew the answer. She was just hoping to ease the girl's nerves.

"Hildy is five. Max is three," she told them.

"Do they live with you full-time?" Valentine wondered.

"Yeah, their dad isn't in the picture anymore."

"That must be hard," Jessie said, "especially with the job situation."

"Which job situation are you talking about?" Bella challenged. "There's more than one."

"I mean with leaving the maid position on the island. How many other jobs do you have?"

"Two right now. That's why I asked you at the door which former employer you talked to—there have been a lot. I work part-time as a cashier at a pharmacy and I pick up shifts as a server at a diner a few blocks over. The maid gig was mostly on weekends, more for the tips than the regular pay. Those guests can be pretty generous."

"How do you manage child care with that schedule?" Jessie asked, legitimately stunned. She could barely manage working while handling a near-adult.

"Hildy just started Kindergarten so that helps. My mom lives in Oakland and tries to juggle her work schedule to help watch Max. There's also a retired neighbor on the second floor who will keep an eye on him when needed. She's sweet, but because of her age, it's hard for her to keep up with him. There's also a daycare drop-in place about a mile away. I only do that as a last resort because it's expensive, even at a reduced rate for financial need. Plus, it always seems like the kids there are sick. I don't want to expose him to that if I can help it."

"That sounds rough," Valentine said sympathetically. "Something pretty bad must have happened for you to be willing to bail on a gig that paid such good tips."

Bella looked at her with exasperation, clearly unimpressed with the clumsy segue.

"I guess this is the part where you explain why the LAPD is knocking on my door at 9:30 on a Monday night," she noted drily. "Was he arrested or something?"

For the first time since they'd arrived, Bella showed a hint of genuine anger. Jessie hardly considered it evidence that she was capable of murder, but it did make her eyes narrow with a bit of suspicion.

"Was who arrested?" she asked, "The guy who did that to you? It depends on who it was."

Bella seemed unsure whether she should answer, but then seemed to mentally say "screw it."

"It was Eddie Morse," she admitted, "The record exec guy who was having the big birthday bash."

Jessie nodded as if she knew it all along.

"How did it happen, Bella?' she asked, keeping her voice soft and using the girl's first name to create a sense of intimacy.

Bella lowered her head for a moment. When she lifted it again, her eyes were hard and set.

"It was last night," she told them, "Sunday, the final night of their visit. All the guests were having dinner in the dining room downstairs. I was doing light cleaning in the suites, making any unmade beds, fluffing pillows, making sure towels and toiletries were well stocked. I was just finishing up the Golden Gate Room, where he and his wife were staying. He came in, saying he forgot his watch."

She stopped briefly and Jessie worried that she might have to prod her, but after a few seconds, she resumed.

"Once he got the watch, I thought he'd leave but he didn't. I knew he'd been drinking all afternoon and could tell he was high out of his mind. He started hitting on me, getting up close, hands wandering. He asked if I would wear a naughty maid outfit for him. I tried to politely talk my way out of it. I mean, the whole point of doing this job is to get good tips, which means not alienating the guests. But he either didn't get it or didn't care. I finally told him flat out that I wasn't interested."

"What happened then?" Jessie asked.

"That's when he slapped me, here," Bella said, pointing to the bruise. "He did it so hard, it actually knocked me down. I was kind of stunned, just sitting there on the ground. I didn't even cry at first. The second it happened, he started apologizing. He helped me up and sat me on the bed. He got some ice and wrapped it in a towel, told me to put it on my cheek. He broke down in tears and said he'd lost control of his life, but that he'd never hit anyone before. He said that it was a sign that he needed help, that he was going to check himself into rehab the next day. Then he told me that he knew it wouldn't make up for what he did, but that when he got off the island the next day, he was going to withdraw some money and give it to me. Then he left the room."

"He just went back down to the dinner?" Valentine asked incredulously.

"I don't know," Bella said. "When I was sure he was gone, I went down the stairs, out the back door, and spent the rest of the night in the staff quarters building. This morning, I decided that I'd had enough. That's when I told the Burns I was quitting. I took the same boat back that Morse was on, along with all the other passengers. I sat with Rita, the other maid, in the corner, praying he didn't come near me. He didn't. I hurried off the boat and caught the bus home. And then, around noon, a courier knocked on my door and had me sign for a package."

"What was in it?" Jessie wanted to know.

"An envelope with $10,000 in cash and a piece of paper with the words 'so sorry' on it. Nothing else."

"What did you do with the money?" Valentine pressed.

"I took it straight to the bank and deposited it. You don't want that kind of money lying around in this neighborhood."

It was a reasonable answer, as all of Bella's had been so far, but it didn't absolve her. Jessie and Valentine were both quiet for a second, well aware that the next question would be difficult. To her credit, Valentine stepped up to ask it.

"Bella, after Eddie Morse left the suite, did you do anything to get even with him, maybe poke a hole in his toothpaste tube or fill his flask with liquid soap or something?"

Bella stared at her, aghast.

"Are you kidding?" she demanded in an angry whisper. "I just wanted to get out of there. Do you really think I'd take the time to play a practical joke on a guy who'd just hit me in the face?"

"So you didn't do anything to get back at him?" Valentine pushed.

"No," Bella insisted emphatically. "I was trapped on an island with the man. I wasn't going to do anything to piss him off again. I just wanted to get away. Why—did he say I did something? Is that why you're here? Did he say I stole something or blackmailed him for the money—because I didn't. I didn't do anything wrong. You should be arresting *him*."

"We can't do that," Jessie said.

"Why not?"

Jessie nodded at Valentine that she could do the honors.

"Because he's dead," Valentine said bluntly, "and we think he was murdered."

Jessie watched Bella's reaction closely. Her previous expression of self-righteous indignation immediately morphed into shock, then confusion, and finally fear.

"What?"

"He died on the private jet that flew him and his friends back to L.A.," Valentine said.

"This happened today?" Bella asked, seemingly still not entirely comprehending the situation.

"That's right, Bella," Jessie said, trying to steady the girl. If she was faking shock, she was very good at it, much too talented an actress to be working multiple low-paying jobs. "And when we learned that he'd withdrawn $10,000 on the morning of his death, just before getting on the jet, we had to follow that up. That's why we're here, to determine if you had anything to with what happened to him."

"How could I?" she asked, straining to keep her volume down with the kids in the next room. "I never interacted with him at all today."

"We think he was poisoned, Bella," Valentine said. "Maybe using the flask he had on him. You're telling us there's no chance you slipped something into that flask as payback for what he did to you?"

She shook her head violently.

"I would never do something like that," she insisted. "Besides, I didn't even know he had a flask. I never saw one."

Jessie glanced over at Valentine, who looked skeptical. It wasn't clear whether that was sincere or for Bella's benefit, to weaken her resolve. Jessie couldn't muster up anything similar. She wouldn't stake her life on it, but she sensed that Bella was telling the truth. They'd need to wait for the test results on the flask to bear that out, but she had a strong feeling that coming to San Francisco may have been a waste of time. Just then, her phone rang. It was Jamil. She looked over at Valentine, who was staring back at her in anticipation.

"I think we're done here," Jessie said.

CHAPTER TWENTY TWO

Jessie could tell Valentine was about to jump out of her skin.

Over the detective's objections, she'd told Jamil to call her back in two minutes, when they could speak freely. After they wrapped up with Bella and left her apartment, they darted down the stairs, Valentine taking the steps two at a time. They had just reached the vestibule near the front door when the call came in.

"What have you got, Jamil?" Jessie asked, putting him on speaker.

"Not much," he said, "the report came back negative. There was no sign of any toxin inside the flask and no fingerprints on the outside besides Morse's. Also, in her notes, the M.E. reiterated what she told you guys—that it's likely that he died within ten to fifteen minutes of ingesting the heroin, maybe sooner."

"Great, so the whole trip up here was pointless," a clearly frustrated Valentine muttered, echoing Jessie's thoughts from earlier. "The chances that anyone not on that plane killed him just dropped to near zero."

"Isn't that a good thing?" Jamil asked. "Now you have a limited pool of suspects to work through, right?"

"That's true," Jessie acknowledged. "I think we were just hoping for a smoking gun. The problem now is that with no cameras on the flight, music blasting at full volume, lights flashing on and off the whole time, and almost everyone on board running around drunk and high, we have no idea who was where when. Unless we catch someone in a lie or one of these folks confesses outright, it's hard to see a path to solving this thing."

"It's dead end after dead end," Valentine grumbled irritably.

"I think we just have to start over," Jessie sighed. "We'll come in to the station tomorrow morning and look at everyone fresh, see if there are contradictions in people's stories that we missed before, unaccounted for time, or quarrels that got nasty. Maybe we'll find a connection that we can't see right now."

"I guess," Valentine said, sounding more like a pouty child than an up-and coming detective.

"Why don't you call it a night too, Jamil? Maybe take Beth out for a celebratory first day drink," Jessie teased. "We're going to head back to the airport. I think that we can still make the 11 p.m. flight you booked us on."

"Okay. See you tomorrow," the researcher said, not commenting on the Beth crack.

"I don't think he appreciates your gentle ribbing," Valentine said, rediscovering her professional tone as they walked out of the apartment building and headed back to the car.

"I just like to get him out of his comfort zone," Jessie said. "He spends so much time behind a screen, I worry that he tends to forget how to handle awkward social situations. So I'm creating a few for him. I'm giving him a gift, really. One day he'll thank me."

"Ten bucks says he files a complaint with HR before he thanks you," Valentine countered as she passed first through the rickety, exterior metal gate leading to the street.

Before Jessie could reply, she suddenly felt an arm wrap around her chest and saw a flash of metal as a knife was shoved up next to her throat.

"Give me all your money," the man holding her growled, "or I'll make you bleed."

Jessie's whole body tensed up as her heart nearly pounded straight through her chest. Valentine quickly turned around. Jessie watched her survey the situation silently.

"Okay," Jessie said, hoping her voice sounded calm despite the anxiety she felt. "Just stay cool. I'll give you what I have but you've got to move that knife away from my neck."

"I'm not moving a thing until I see cash," the guy insisted. Though Jessie couldn't see him well from her angle, now that she'd had a moment to breathe, she realized that her attacker was more of a boy than a man. He was much shorter than her, his voice was high, and out of the corner of her eye, she could see that his face was smooth. He didn't even have peach fuzz yet. She guessed he was thirteen or fourteen at the most.

"You don't want to do this, young man," Valentine said, confirming Jessie's suspicion about his age. "This is armed robbery. You could go to prison for a long time."

"Only if I get caught," he shot back, "Now you shut up while your friend here gives me her money."

Valentine's right hand drifted down casually, as if she was just resting it on her hip, but when it stopped, it ended up next to her gun holster.

"You need to loosen your grip a little so I can get to my wallet," Jessie said, hoping to distract him from her partner.

"Don't you worry about me," the kid demanded, pressing the blade harder against her neck. She winced as it broke the skin. "Just get your damn money out, lady."

"Okay," Jessie said soothingly. "I'm reaching for my wallet. Just stay calm."

There was no way she could go for her gun. By the time she got it out, he'd have slit her throat twice over. But she got the sense that he didn't want to do that. She pulled out her folded over department ID, which looked like a traditional wallet on the outside, and extended it out in front of her, beyond his reach.

"Does your mom know you're doing this?" she asked quietly. "Would she be proud of you right now?"

"What?" he asked, taken aback, his eyes shifting from the ID back to her.

It was in that moment that Susannah Valentine, in one fluid motion, unholstered her weapon and pointed it the kid. When he looked back at her, the gun was trained on his face.

"You're going to want to drop the knife," she said forcefully. "I don't miss too often from under ten feet away."

Jessie felt the kid's arm shake a little as his nerves got the better of him. The blade scraped at her neck but she said nothing.

"Who are you?" he asked in a hushed voice.

"You want to let him know who we are, Jessie?" Valentine asked loudly. "Show him that ID your holding."

Jessie obliged, letting the ID unfold to reveal her identification as a consulting profiler for the Los Angeles Police Department, complete with the department logo. She felt him twitch as he processed what he was looking at.

"We're LAPD, friend," Valentine said coolly. "You picked the wrong ladies to mess with. So this can go one of two ways for you: not great or truly awful. Your best bet is to lay the knife on the ground and put your hands up. You're clearly a juvenile. If you don't push this any farther, you might get off easy. But if you do anything else, you won't be around to have to worry about juvie. I don't want anyone to die here tonight. But if my partner does, so do you, only not before I blow holes in both your knees, your shoulders and your baby-making parts. Am I making myself clear?"

The kid was frozen in place. Jessie could hear his shallow breathing and feel the vibrations of his quaking body. But he still hadn't dropped the knife.

"I think you know the right move here," she whispered to him. "My partner doesn't seem to be in much of a negotiating mood."

She had barely gotten the words out when he snapped into action. Without warning, he shoved her forward hard toward Valentine. As she tried to keep her balance and keep from falling, the detective stepped forward and steadied her with her non-gun hand. Once she'd regrouped, Jessie spun around to see the kid sprinting off toward the darkness beyond the part building.

"Don't shoot," she said.

They both watched as he disappeared into the shadows. Even after he was gone, they could hear his sneakers squeaking as they faded into the distance. Valentine let go of her.

"I wasn't going to shoot him after he let you go," she said, sounding offended. "What kind of cop do you think I am?"

Jessie reached up to touch the spot where he'd held the knife against her neck. When she checked her hand, it was slightly red. She looked at Valentine.

"I'm still trying to figure that out," she said.

"Well let me help you out," Valentine shot back. "For one, I'm the kind of cop who just saved your life."

Jessie could feel the situation, which was already heightened, escalating more, and realized it was on her to rein things back in. She slowly pulled a tissue out of her pocket and dabbed at the raw spot.

"Thank you for that," she said, "And again for what you did earlier on the wharf."

Her words seemed to slightly mute Valentine's anger. She looked like she was about to come back at her again but stopped herself.

"I'm doing the best I can here," she finally said. "I don't know why you're giving me such a hard time."

Jessie was mildly stunned by the comment. She thought about mentioning the detective's overbearing interrogation technique, her need to always be right, even when she was wrong, not to mention her repeated attempts to seduce Ryan in front of everyone in the unit. Considering all that, Jessie thought she was being pretty restrained.

Despite the multiple black marks against her, the fact remained that twice in the last two hours, Susannah Valentine had saved her life. That deserved some kind of pass, at least for the rest of the night.

"I appreciate you stopping that kid from slicing my head off my body. And preventing my bones from getting crushed to dust by that boat was a real solid. You should be proud of your work tonight, Susannah."

It pained her to use the woman's first name, but it obviously made a huge difference to Valentine, who blushed and had to fight back a smile.

"Yeah, well," she said, trying to sound offhand and failing, "we should probably get going if we're going to catch that flight. I want to sleep in my own bed tonight."

Jessie did too. She wanted to see her family, to check on Ryan's ankle and, most of all, to find out what the hell was going on with Hannah. With all that in mind, she opened the car door.

"Then we better get going."

CHAPTER TWENTY THREE

Andy Robinson got lucky.

The Western Regional Women's Psychiatric Detention Center didn't usually allow patients to make calls this late. Lights out at the PDC was at 10 p.m. and it was already 9:52. But with her transfer yesterday and all the associated paperwork and chaos, she'd been denied her official "first night" authorized call to a friend or loved one.

She'd already determined which attendant would be the easiest to manipulate and waited until he was alone to make her pitch. She came at him hard.

"This place was supposed to better than the last one I was at, but you're already violating my rights as a patient and a prisoner," she said loudly, her voice echoing in the empty hallway. "Who do I need to file a complaint with?"

It worked like a charm. The attendant, named Dewey, hurried her to the call area before her grievance escalated and pleaded with the security guard on duty to make an exception for him. As a result, she was now directed to a tiny room about twice the size of a phone booth.

"You're permitted one call," Dewey told her, "and it can't last more than three minutes."

"Understood, Dewey," she said with a smile. She wouldn't need half that.

It was time to put phase two of her plan into action. Phase one had worked perfectly. She had groomed and manipulated a group of inmates back at Twin Towers for months, including a pathetic, malleable sad sack of a patient named Livia Bucco. She trained them all in what she called "The Principles."

To Livia and her other minions, The Principles were a series of life instructions to follow religiously, designed by her. They included seemingly constructive rules like: always remember that your mind is your strongest tool. It can take you anywhere if you let it. Another was: Don't betray a sister in need; be ready to help a sister complete her deed.

But first among the rules was the Primary Principle: Protect the Principal, as in never reveal the identity of the group's leader or her teachings, even if it means sacrificing yourself to keep the secret.

To the women incarcerated with Andy, this was a creed to live by and she was their prophet, giving them hope and providing meaning to their confused worlds. They were troubled, unstable, vulnerable people and having something important to cling to bred intense loyalty to the person who made that feeling possible.

So if she asked them to commit a crime when they were released from the overcrowded facility where they'd been held, they didn't consider it a burden but an honor, a way to prove their worth to the group and especially to her. Of course, to Andy, these Principles were merely a means to her specific end—to win back Jessie Hunt's trust. She didn't buy into them at all. In fact, she'd modeled her leadership style after Tyler Durden in the movie, *Fight Club*. The Primary Principle—Protect the Principal—was really just a variation on "don't talk about Fight Club." Apparently these idiots had never seen the movie.

The first to put the Principles into action was Livia Bucco. When she was released from Twin Towers two weeks ago, she had burned Andy's instructions into her brain: take the machete her father had left her when he died and butcher an innocent person in a shocking location. Then do the same thing again the next day. If you're ever in danger of getting captured by the authorities, sacrifice your life for the greater good and become a martyr to the cause.

That's exactly what Livia did, finding a kindhearted law student who was providing legal aid at a local YWCA and butchering the girl while she was showering after a swim at the facility. Once it happened, Andy reached out to Jessie to tell her she thought the killer was a former inmate she knew and gave her up name, which allowed the cops to find Livia, only to watch her kill herself before they could arrest her.

It had all worked beautifully. Livia had gone to her death keeping Andy's identity secret. Even better, Jessie was indebted to her and agreed to help facilitate her transfer to PDC in exchange for additional information she might glean about crimes committed by others she had met in lockup.

But for her to help solve crimes, there had to be crimes, and that's what this phone call was about. Two weeks had gone by without her trade currency: a senseless murder committed by a mental patient released too early because of overcrowding and budget cuts. It was time to rev things up again and create some havoc that would have Jessie back at her knee, begging for help.

So she made her pre-arranged call. The phone rang twice before a female voice picked up.

"Downes residence."

"Hello ma'am," Andy said, using the agreed-upon title, "it's Andrea Robinson. I just wanted to let you know that I'm settling in at the new place. I wanted to thank you for all your support."

"Of course, dear," the woman on the other end of the line said.

"As I mentioned in our final session, I promise to keep you updated on how I'm doing. But I know it's getting late tonight so maybe the next time I'll call in the afternoon, around 3 p.m. Would that be okay?"

"I think I can make that work," the other woman said. "You go ahead and do that and we can check in on how things are going for you."

"I really appreciate it, ma'am. Talk again soon." Andy replied, managing to include a hint of choked up emotion in her voice. She knew the call was being recorded and thought the moment might play well when it was inevitably listened to later.

After she hung up, she stayed in the phone booth an extra minute so its brevity didn't seem suspicious. The privacy gave her a moment to review how the call had gone. It seemed to be a success. The number she'd dialed was for one of her psychiatrists back at Twin Towers, an older woman named Dr. Loretta Downes, who had to leave her position at the facility several months ago after getting diagnosed with Alzheimer's.

Of course, Andy had noticed her condition well before the prison hospital authorities did. That advantage came in handy when she subsequently met the doctor's granddaughter, Scarlett, a student at USC studying abnormal psychology, who was visiting the prison to see her grandma and observe patients.

Andy and Scarlett hit it off during one of the many sessions when Dr. Downes spent long stretches staring blankly into the distance. It didn't take long for Scarlett's fascination with Andy to turn into adoration. Within a month of that first visit, Scarlett was under her spell.

But Scarlett Downes was far too valuable to use as merely a one-time creator of murderous mayhem. Andy had her move in with her grandma in anticipation of this very moment—when she could call Dr. Downes for a friendly chat but instead secretly pass instructions to Scarlett, who would then convey them to current or former inmates at the Twin Towers.

In her time there, Andy had cultivated six devotees, not including Scarlett. All had specific assignments to complete when called upon. All had sworn allegiance to her and the Principles she had given them.

110

Three had already been released, including the unfortunate Livia. One was slated for imminent discharge. Two more could be free within a few months, depending on good behavior.

Andy had assigned each of them a number. When she mentioned calling again at 3 p.m., that was code for Scarlett to activate #3 on the list of devotees. Number 3 was a lovely, frail, young thing named Eden Roth, who had been living a quiet, unassuming life for almost eight months now. It would be difficult to connect her to Andy in any real way, and therefore, hard to suggest that Eden's impending act of violence could be traced to her.

If all went well, Scarlett would contact Eden within the next twenty-four hours and Andy would see the fruits of her careful inculcation within a week of that. Andy was giddy. This was her first attempt to do the mental hospital version of activating a sleeper agent. It was exciting. Once the chaos started up, it shouldn't be long before Jessie came to her for help.

But there was more work to do. Eventually the supply of adherents from Twin Towers would start to deplete. That's why she needed to develop new assets here at the PDC. It might take months for Jessie to really warm up to her again. And until she did, Andy needed a steady supply of mental patient cannon fodder to provide good case material for the profiler. She would begin that work tomorrow.

Andy stood up and opened the door to the phone room, where both Dewey the attendant and the security guard were waiting.

"Thanks for giving me the time," she said sweetly. "I'm ready to go back now."

"So we're all good?" Dewey asked hesitantly, not wanting to deal with any more threats of filing grievances.

"We're great, Dewey. And hopefully tomorrow will be even better."

CHAPTER TWENTY FOUR

Jessie's eyelids felt like weighted blankets.

By the time she pulled into the garage back home, it was almost 1 a.m. Only a combination of wide open windows and belting out duets with an unknowing Kelly Clarkson got her through the drive back from the airport.

Once she'd locked everything up, she poked her head into Hannah's room. Her sister was splayed out on her bed. She had kicked off her blankets at some point. It was in the forties tonight and Jessie was tempted to sneak in and put them back on her, but the fear of waking her was too strong, so she left her alone.

One she got into her bedroom, she saw Ryan lying on his back, snoring gently. She snuck into the bathroom and washed up as quietly as possible. But when she got into bed, she saw that he was awake.

"Sorry," she whispered as she pulled the covers over her.

"That's okay," he muttered. "I wanted to make sure you got home safe."

"Safe and sound," she assured him, making no mention of her two brushes with death. "How were things here?"

"Could be better," he said sleepily. "I finally confronted Hannah about all her crap—her attitude toward you, worrying us with her behavior, refusing to tell Dr. Lemmon about the whole 'killing a guy' thing. I'm not sure it did any good."

"Oh wow," Jessie said apprehensively. "I guess we'll find out more tomorrow. Thanks for taking a stand."

"I was just sick of it, you know," he yawned. "I know I'm not technically her guardian, but I'm not just some silent observer either."

"No," she agreed. "You have a say too and I'm glad you said something."

"How did things go up north?" he asked, trying to keep his droopy eyes open.

"Don't worry about it," she said. "I can fill you in tomorrow."

"At least give me the basics," he insisted.

Jessie stared up at the ceiling, trying to decide how to even begin.

"Well, we know Morse was intentionally given an overdose of heroin, but we weren't sure when. We were hoping that a visit to the island where his group stayed for his birthday weekend might reveal something definitive. But after multiple interviews and nearly throwing up on a boat in the middle of the ocean, we got word that the amount of heroin was so massive that it would have had to have been slipped to him on the plane. So the trip was a bust. No one there could have done it. Now we're back to the drawing board. I'm not sure what we're missing. I feel like the solution to this is within my grasp but then it fades away. It's like my intuition has abandoned me on this one, you know?"

Ryan's response came in the form of another soft snore. She took her eyes off the ceiling and glanced over at him. He was out. She wasn't sure exactly when she lost him but she couldn't blame him. Just like this case had her running in circles, now she was talking in them too.

She sighed and closed her own eyes, hoping the events of the day wouldn't keep her up thinking too late. She needn't have worried as she was asleep less than a minute later.

*

Jessie knew Ryan was in the station break room and headed there, hoping she might be able sneak up and playfully goose him. To her surprise, the blinds to the room were closed and it looked like the lights were off too. Confused and worried that something was wrong, she tiptoed the rest of the way.

When she opened the door, the light from the hall streamed in, casting a glow on two people at the far end of the room. Susannah Valentine had her back pressed up to the refrigerator in the corner. Her top was unbuttoned and someone had his arms wrapped around her waist with his head burrowed against her neck, his face hidden by her wildly mussed, black hair.

Valentine noticed the light from the hall where Jessie stood and looked that way. When she saw who was in the doorway, she quickly tapped the man entwined with her on the shoulder and pointed at Jessie. He looked over. It was Ryan. He looked briefly startled to see her. But then, without a word, he turned back to Valentine and resumed what he was doing. Valentine gave Jessie a contented smile and called out to her.

"Can you shut the door please?"

*

Jessie's eyes snapped open. She was staring at her bedroom ceiling. Ryan was still beside her in bed, snoring softly. She looked at the clock. It was 3:40 a.m. Ignoring the beads of sweat on her forehead, she took several deep breaths, hoping to clear her head and drift back to sleep.

An hour later she was still awake.

CHAPTER TWENTY FIVE

By the time Jessie woke up, Ryan was gone.

After she let the brief, inevitable moment of panic pass, she looked over at the clock. It was 7:38. Ryan must have turned off her alarm so she could get some more sleep.

Glancing over to his side of the bed, she saw a note on the pillow. It read: *Decker called. Insisted that you not come in before nine, so I reset your alarm. Don't be pissed. My ankle feels much better. Going in today. Will drop off Hannah at school on the way. I love you.*

She got up slowly, happy that she didn't have to rush to get into the office. She had just gotten in the shower when it occurred to her that neither Valentine nor Jamil would follow Decker's instructions about getting extra sleep. The realization that she might end up being the slacker who rolled in last kicked her into high gear.

Sure enough, when she arrived at the station at 8:30, Valentine was already staring at her computer screen, hard at work. Jessie noted that while she looked gorgeously immaculate after so little sleep, she didn't appear to have just come from a secret tryst. Her top was completely buttoned up and her hair was nicely groomed. Detective Jim Nettles was nearby, typing away at something, his eyes on his keyboard instead of the screen. Ryan was nowhere to be found.

"Morning," Jessie said to them both. "What's the word?"

"Oh good, you're here," Valentine said, as if she'd been waiting for hours. "Jamil is in the research office with Beth. They've been working on a special project they want us to see. You ready to head back there?"

"Sure," Jessie replied, "Any idea where Ryan is?"

Nettles looked up from his keyboard.

"Decker assigned him and Karen Bray a case about a half hour ago," he said. "He asked me to give you this when you got in. He said you should eat it in lieu of the breakfast you almost certainly didn't have when you rushed out of the house this morning."

He handed her an apple cinnamon and sunflower butter breakfast protein bar. As far as crappy, on-the-go breakfasts went, it was her favorite. Her fiancé really did know her well. She felt a sudden rush of guilt about the aspersions her unconscious mind had cast on him last night.

Sneaking a sideways glance at Valentine, she felt less guilty about any negative thoughts she had about her. They headed to the research department together. Jessie used eating the protein bar as an excuse not to talk.

"You sleep okay?" Valentine asked.

"Mmm hmm," Jessie mumbled with a full mouth, pointing back at the detective to ask the same thing.

"Okay, I guess," she replied. "I had a hard time getting settled. My mind kept racing, playing out different scenarios of what might have happened on that plane. I couldn't shut it down."

They rounded the corner and stepped into the research room. No one was there. But as Jessie looked around, she immediately noticed that the large whiteboard on the wall had been turned into a suspect board, and was completely covered in pictures and notes.

Jessie walked over to get a closer look. The pictures were of each person on the flight yesterday, with arrows showing their connections to each other and to Morse, as well as timelines of their whereabouts that morning and during the prior weekend. The work was impressively comprehensive, though there were a lot of red question marks.

"They've been busy," Valentine marveled.

"You have no idea," someone said from behind them.

They turned around to find Jamil standing there with a cup of coffee in his hand, Next to him was a tall brunette in slacks, a nice blouse, and a sports jacket. Beth Ryerson looked more like a lawyer leaving court than a police researcher.

Jessie tried not to crack a smile at the sight of her. Though they appeared to be about the same age, Beth was the physical antithesis of Jamil. He was short and, though he'd been working out lately, still thin to the point of near-scrawniness. Beth wasn't just taller than Jamil; she was taller than Jessie, easily over six feet. She had the formidable look of a former volleyball player, which Jessie suspected she might have been. Her long legs and muscled shoulders suggested she had taken it seriously.

She was pretty in a "don't give a damn" way, with her brown hair pulled back in a loose ponytail and virtually no makeup on. She wore thin glasses that only added to her disarming energy. Jessie liked her immediately.

"You must be Beth," she said, extending her hand.

"Nice to officially meet you, ma'am—er, Jessie," Beth said, remembering the instruction from yesterday, "And nice to see you too, Detective Valentine."

Valentine gave her a tight smile. It seemed the only person in the office she liked to joke around with was Ryan.

"Where do you play?" Jessie asked.

"I'm sorry?" Beth asked.

"Volleyball," Jessie prompted. "Did you just play in high school or college too?'

"Both," Beth said, blushing. "I was an outside hitter at UC-Santa Barbara."

"Very cool," Jessie said. "And now you've brought your competitive spirit to the world of crime-fighting. Glad to have you aboard."

"Thanks very much," she said, her face getting even redder. "How did you kn—?"

"Care to explain what we've got up here?" Valentine asked sharply, cutting the moment short.

"Yes, right," Jamil said quickly, putting down his coffee and moving over to the whiteboard. "We spent much of last night and part of this morning reviewing your interviews from the jet hangar yesterday, along with what we could piece together from the GPS data from everyone's phone. We believe we've put together a preliminary timetable of where everyone was during the weekend."

"As you can see from the many question marks," Beth said, picking up where Jamil left off, "there are a lot of gaps. Since the island is so small and everyone spent most of their time in the bed & breakfast complex, a lot of their location data overlaps. We reached out to Barney and Sally Burns this morning and were able to get a little clarity based on some additional information they provided about who participated in certain activities over the course of the weekend."

"Like what?" Valentine asked.

"Well, they had a fishing outing every afternoon. There were multiple seal and bird watching sessions. Guests would tally numbers and classify birds, and then submit them to the Burns, who would report the data to the nonprofit that runs the place for the Coast Guard. Plus, we were able to access some phone data on the actual flight back to L.A. to determine when specific people were making calls or active online. It's far from comprehensive, but it might be helpful."

Jessie stared at the board and realized that, if nothing else, it might help them determine if anyone was lying about where they were at a specific time. It would require a lot of painstaking work and it might not reveal the identity of the killer. But if they could catch someone in a lie, they could put pressure on that person. And pressure usually led to revelations they might not otherwise get. It was better than what she thought they had when she woke up this morning.

"This is great work, guys," she said. "Unfortunately, for it to help us, I think we're in for a lot more work. I'm going to grab a coffee too. We might be here a while."

*

Nearly three hours later, they were still at it.

They'd made lots of connections and managed to change a number of question marks on the board into actual times and places, but nothing they'd uncovered revealed anyone in the group of suspects to be more than the boorish, entitled, greedy, covetous, drug-addled trolls they'd already shown themselves to be. Almost nothing, that is.

Jessie was just finishing her third cup of coffee when something she'd missed earlier caught her attention. She walked up close to the board to make sure she was seeing it correctly. As it became clear to her that this discovery was new, she turned to face the group excitedly.

"Is it just me or does it look like neither Eddie Morse nor Vivien Baldwin are accounted for in the late afternoon on Sunday?"

The others looked at the board. Jamil started rifling through his notes. Beth did the same before looking up suddenly.

"According to the Burns' log of activities, you may be right," she said. "Between 4:30 and 5:15, everyone else was either seal-watching or on a wildlife walk around the island."

"And during that time," Jamil added. "The phone GPS data for both Eddie and Vivien shows them static in the general vicinity of the inn."

"That doesn't automatically mean there was anything suspicious going on with them," Valentine cautioned.

"No," Jessie agreed, "but in my interview with her at the hangar, I remember Vivien saying she enjoyed the wildlife walk. And from what I can tell, they only held that activity one time all weekend, on Sunday afternoon. So either the Burns forgot to include her on the list, or she was lying."

Jamil's fingers flew across his keyboard.

"I just re-confirmed it," he said. "Her GPS data doesn't show her wandering around at that time. The phone never moves, at least not enough to register."

"Maybe she just left it in her room," Beth suggested. "You said there was no signal on the island. What would be the point of taking it with her?"

Now Valentine's face lit up.

"You'd think she'd want to take pictures on a wildlife walk," she noted. "And unless she was an avid photographer and had a fancy camera, she'd probably just take them on her phone."

"So if she was lying about the wildlife walk," Jessie mused, "the question is why."

Jamil, who had never stopped typing the whole time they were talking, suddenly lifted his hands off the keyboard.

"I don't know the answer to that question," he said. "But I do have another tidbit that you might find interesting."

"What's that?" Valentine asked.

"Until four years ago, Vivien Baldwin worked for a pharmaceutical company based in Woodland Hills. And from what I can tell, she's still in regular contact with people there. Is it conceivable that she might know how to access large quantities of diacetylmorphine?"

Jessie turned back to Valentine, who seemed to be actually smiling.

"What do you say, Detective," she asked. "Shall we pay another visit to Mrs. Baldwin?"

She had barely finished the question when Valentine started for the door.

"I'll take that as a yes."

CHAPTER TWENTY SIX

Hannah imagined that this was what it must be like for a ghost.

As she sat in the busy courtyard outside her high school cafeteria just after noon, watching kids at nearby tables enjoying Taco Tuesday, she felt invisible, observing events without participating.

She sat alone at the table, waiting for her friends, who were in line inside. She had offered to save a table since she wasn't hungry. Ever since she'd woken up this morning, there was a raw pit of emptiness in her gut that wouldn't go away. It had taken a while to figure out what it was, but sitting by herself, bundled up against the February chill, with laughing people everywhere around her, it came to her in a flash: she felt guilty.

It was such a rare emotion for her that it wasn't always easy to identify. But she couldn't get out of her head what Ryan, who had never called her out before, said last night. She couldn't forget the pain in his eyes as he reminded her how much Jessie had sacrificed for her.

It was true. Jessie Hunt had been a stranger to her not very long ago. Now she was the most important person in her life, someone who had stood by her when there was no one else, who had taken her in and restructured her whole world around a damaged teenage girl. She was her big sister. And despite all of that, Hannah couldn't do the one thing her sister had asked of her, to tell her therapist about what had happened that snowy night in Wildpines.

Hannah's friends walked over with their lunch trays. As they did, she stood up. She'd come to a decision.

"Thanks for saving the table," Holly said.

"Don't worry about it," Hannah said distractedly. "I'm actually not feeling great. Can you tell Mr. Martin that I had to go home?"

"Okay," Holly said, "But you should go to the nurse first or else it'll be an unexcused absence."

"I don't have the time to deal with the hassle," Hannah said. "I'll just handle it tomorrow."

"But if you try to leave campus without a note from the nurse, security will nail you," Holly reminded her.

"You know me," Hannah said, trying not to roll her eyes. "When's the last time I worried about what a security guard would do?"

She left before waiting for an answer, requesting a ride share as she walked from the courtyard toward the back of the school, near the teachers' parking lot, which wasn't as heavily patrolled as other areas. The driver would be there in two minutes.

She looked around. There was no security in sight. Nonetheless, she unslung her backpack, which was a telltale sign that someone was a student, and held it in her hand like a briefcase as she walked briskly toward the back of the parking lot. She was halfway there when she heard a voice call out from behind her.

Turning around, she saw an older gentleman in a guard uniform walking toward her. It was Phil, who was deliberately kept out of high student traffic areas because he tended to get overwhelmed by the crowds. She was ninety-five percent sure he had no idea who she was.

"Can I help you, young lady?" he asked wheezily.

"Young lady?" she repeated, laughing appreciatively. "That's sweet, Phil, but we both know that I barely deserve that designation anymore. After all, I'm closer to thirty than to twenty now."

"Aren't you a student?" he asked, perplexed.

She laughed even louder this time.

"You are adorable," she said. "I know I'm just a substitute teacher, but please tell me you don't really think I'm still in high school? At least tell me I look like a senior, Phil. Come on, I'm Ms. King, Cheryl King. I'm teaching 9th grade English this week while Ms. Whitmore is at her father's funeral back in Tuscaloosa."

"But you don't have a substitute badge on?" he said uncertainly.

"Oh dear," she said, touching her shirt. "I guess I must have left it in the room. In any case, my ride just pulled up. I have to run to the pharmacy real quick before the start of 4th period. Back in a jiff, Phil."

She turned and continued walking to the waiting car, hoping that Phil wouldn't call after her. Even if he did, she wasn't stopping. By the time, she reached car door, he'd said nothing. She got in without looking back.

*

Dr. Janice Lemmon's stomach was grumbling. She had just walked out the front door of her building in search of food when she almost collided into Hannah Dorsey.

"My goodness," she said, reaching out to the younger girl to stop from tripping. "What a surprise to see you here, Hannah. I believe we were supposed to meet yesterday. Did we have another session that I forgot about?"

"No," Hannah said, seemingly unprepared to see her. "It's just…"

Her voice trailed off. Janice took a step back and studied the young woman. She looked frazzled in a way that was rare for her. Her body language was tense and her eyes were filled with a level of self-doubt that was usually absent.

Something was up. Janice wondered if it might be the same thing that had been eating at the girl for over a month, the revelation that she had almost shared over FaceTime from a coffeehouse two weeks ago. She looked to be on the verge. But she'd looked that way before.

"I was just stepping out to get a bite," Janice said, not wanting to push it. "Have you eaten? Would you like to join me?"

Hannah nodded wordlessly. Janice had been planning to go to her favorite diner. But it was always busy and that didn't feel right at the moment. Instead, they walked the half block to a little café she knew had a quiet table in a back nook of the place. Once they arrived, she requested the table and the greeter led them back. Only when they were alone, did Janice finally speak again.

"If you're into it, they have a great tuna melt here," she suggested, waiting for Hannah to get down to business. It didn't take long.

"We have a doctor patient privilege, right?" she asked. "You can't reveal what I tell you in a session?"

"In general, yes," Janice assured her. "There are some exceptions but if you're worried that I'm telling Jessie about the contents of our discussions, I'm not."

"No, it's not that," Hannah said. "Can you tell the authorities what I say?"

"It depends," Janice said. "Let me ask you this—does your sister know what you intend to reveal to me?"

"Yes."

"Did she suggest you not do so?"

"No," Hannah said. "She wants me to tell you."

"In that case, you can feel reasonably comfortable. I don't think Jessie would advise you to tell me something that could put you at legal risk. But to be safe, let's agree that our time here is a formal session and not just two impossibly beautiful women having a nice lunch, all right?"

Hannah nodded. The server came over.

"Can you give us a few minutes please?" Janice asked. "I'll let you know when to come back."

The server left. Hannah glanced back to make sure she was out of earshot and then did it a second time to reconfirm their privacy. When she seemed sure they couldn't be heard, she turned back around. After a long sigh, she spoke.

"You know the Night Hunter, the serial killer I shot when Jessie, Ryan, and I were in hiding up in Wildpines last month?" she asked.

"I do."

"It wasn't self-defense," Hannah whispered, her eyes fixed on the table between them as the words spilled out rapidly. "Jessie and Ryan had already caught him. He was handcuffed and on the floor. But he started threatening to keep coming after us. I got angry. But there was more. I was curious about…I've always wondered…I realized that if I shot him, it wasn't likely that anything would happen to me, considering all the crimes he'd committed, how reviled he was. So I shot him."

She stopped for a moment but Janice knew she wasn't done and said nothing. A moment later, Hannah started up again.

"I shot him in the chest, but not just because I was mad. It was also because I wanted to kill a person. I wanted to know what it felt like. And you know what? It felt good. Better than good. It was euphoric. My brain tingled. It was more powerful than I could have ever imagined."

Janice sat quietly for several seconds before responding.

"Is that what you wanted to tell me all this time?" she asked, sensing that there was more.

"Partly," Hannah replied. "But that's not all of it. I know it was wrong, even if he was a monster. I could tell that Jessie and Ryan were horrified, even though the man had been trying to kill all of us moments earlier. But here's the thing that really gets me, Dr. Lemmon: after the euphoria faded, I missed it. I wanted to get that feeling back again. I still do. And I don't know what to do with that."

Dr. Janice Lemmon wasn't sure what to say. In all her years of therapy, she'd never had a client tell her flat out that she'd killed someone to find out what it felt like and enjoyed it so much that she wanted that feeling back. To stall, she motioned for the server to come over.

"May I have a cup of tea please?" she requested before turning to Hannah, "Anything for you?"

The girl shook her head. She looked lost. Once the server left, Janice knew she couldn't wait any longer. She chose her words carefully.

"That's a lot, Hannah," she said. "It's no wonder you've had so much trouble sharing this. It must have been such a burden on you. I'm going to try to help you, okay?"

"I'd like that," Hannah said with more sincerity than Janice had ever heard from her.

But even as she made sure her expression didn't betray her thoughts, her mind was racing. She had expected that Hannah's disclosure would be significant but she could never have imagined this. The girl was basically telling her that she was a loaded gun itching to go off.

"We'll figure something out," she said reassuringly.

That seemed to calm Hannah. But Janice wasn't entirely sure that what she'd said was true. Admittedly, there was an option that came to mind, one that might help enormously. The problem was that it could also do incredible damage.

Like a cure that was sometimes worse than the disease, this option could save Hannah Dorsey, but it might also break her forever.

CHAPTER TWENTY SEVEN

Jessie didn't hear any yacht rock playing this time around.

Vivien answered the front door when she and Valentine arrived at her Marina del Rey mansion.

"Back so soon?" she asked amiably, as if they were all old friends now.

"We have a few more questions for you, if you don't mind," Valentine said. "Is your husband around?"

"Nope," Vivien said loudly. Jessie realized that even though it was only 12:35, the woman was drunk again. "He's off trying to salvage an unsalvageable company. He might be gone a while."

"May we come in?" Jessie asked, pretending not to notice the woman's compromised state.

"Be my guest," Vivien said, opening the door wide. "Come in and I'll get you some tea, or if you prefer, a white wine spritzer."

She led them inside, down a long hallway decorated with nautical equipment, including multiple wall-mounted ship wheels and several box-framed, old-timey compasses, cross staffs, and astrolabes. The hall opened into a large, airy living room with floor to ceiling windows that allowed for an unobstructed view of the marina.

She motioned for them to take seats on the plush, cream and teal colored couch. She sat opposite them on a cushy matching loveseat and took a sip of the drink she'd left on the nearby end table.

"Anything for you ladies?" she asked, holding out her glass.

Both women shook their heads.

"So to what do I owe the honor?" she asked before taking another sip.

"We're just trying to clear a few things up about the timeline of events on the island," Jessie said casually. "For example, where were you on Sunday in the late afternoon to early evening timeframe?"

Vivien scrunched up her face as if struggling to remember.

"It's all kind of a blur," she said. "The island wasn't that big. I didn't really keep track of where I was at any given time and it's all starting to fade in my memory anyway. Is that bad?"

Valentine leaned in and when she spoke, Jessie was impressed that her tone was conspiratorial rather than accusatory.

125

"It's just that when we were reviewing everybody's interviews from the jet hangar, you mentioned that you went on the scheduled wildlife walk around that time."

"Oh yeah, that sounds right," Vivien said, though she didn't look entirely convinced of her own words.

"That's what's a little weird though," Valentine continued, "Because no one saw you on that walk and your phone's geo-location shows you being at the inn during that time."

"Huh?" Vivien replied, not sure how to respond.

Jessie didn't volunteer that her partner was playing a little fast and loose with the truth. While the geo-location did show that her phone was in the general area of the inn rather than moving around the island, it couldn't get more nuanced than that. Her phone simply appeared as a big dot that could have been in the courtyard next to the inn, in the lighthouse tower, or essentially anywhere in the bed & breakfast complex. But that wasn't the impression the detective was giving.

"The funny thing is," Valentine continued, "that the only other guest whose geo-location data shows them at the inn around that time was Eddie. What's up with that?"

"Oh yeah," Vivien said, visibly uncomfortable for the first time as she shifted on the loveseat, "Now I remember, we were both inside and chatting it up."

"Then why did you say you were on the wildlife walk?" Valentine wondered, sounding a little less amiable than before.

Vivien put down her drink and did her best to focus on the woman who was pressing her.

"I guess I got confused," she said slowly. "I have to ask: what does any of this have to do with Eddie's death?"

Jessie and Valentine exchanged a glance. They both knew this moment was coming but now that it was here, neither was sure how best to broach it. Other than Barney Burns and the maid, Bella Cammareri, they hadn't revealed to anyone under suspicion that Eddie had been murdered.

Telling Vivien Baldwin now almost certainly meant that it would spread among the others in their group. But there wasn't much choice at this point. Jessie nodded, silently indicating that she would take the lead. To her surprise, Valentine didn't object.

"Vivien," she said, fixing the woman with a stern stare. "Eddie didn't die of an overdose on the jet. He was murdered with a massive dose of powdered heroin mixed into his drink. He was basically poisoned."

She watched the woman closely, gauging her reaction to the news. Vivien blinked several times, as if the words had been said in a foreign language, one that she didn't understand. She seemed genuinely surprised, though she might have been preparing for this moment.

"What?" she finally asked.

"Eddie was murdered," Jessie repeated, "and we're trying to find out who did it. That's why what happened on the island is important. And that's why we need you to tell us what happened when the two of you chatted at the bed & breakfast when everyone else was gone."

Vivien looked over at Valentine as if she might tell her that this was all a terrible joke. When the detective did no such thing, she turned back to Jessie.

"Um, it might look bad," she said hesitantly. "Under the circumstances, I'm not sure I want to talk about it."

"I have to tell you," Jessie replied, "not talking is what really looks bad. You're probably better off telling us your version of events before someone else does."

Vivien seemed to be weighing her options. Jessie decided to give her an extra little push.

"Were you and Eddie sleeping together?" she asked.

Vivien slumped in her seat and the answer was obvious before she said a word.

"That's the ironic thing," she finally replied, closing her eyes as she spoke. "We weren't, at least not on that occasion."

"What does that mean?" Valentine pressed, a little harder than Jessie might have liked.

Vivien opened her eyes again and they were brimming with tears.

"We'd been having an on-and-off-again affair for a couple of years now. It started on a group Swiss ski trip a couple of Christmases ago and kept going after that. It eventually became more than just physical. But the prospect of getting serious was too scary so we both broke it off several times, saying it had to end. But neither of us really believed that and we'd always hook up again. It was the perfect indiscretion for both of us because we each had too much to lose if it got out. It would have been mutually assured destruction. Besides, we couldn't stay away from each other."

"Except for this weekend?" Jessie asked.

"Yes," she replied emphatically. "That what we were talking about. Despite how it would blow everything up, he'd told me repeatedly in the past that he planned to leave Patricia. That's what I wanted too and I kind of cornered him in their suite and demanded that he fish or cut

127

bait. But he said that we had to break it off, for good this time. He said that Patricia had caught him in the act with some coat check girl a few nights earlier and that had snapped him out of it. He loved his wife. He couldn't lose her. He said he promised her that he'd turn over a new leaf, once and for all, and that meant we were done. I knew he was serious this time."

"How did you know?" Jessie asked.

"Because he was sober when he told me. And Eddie was very rarely sober."

Jessie made no mention of the fact that Eddie's "new leaf" plan didn't last all that long, considering that he accosted and assault Bella later that same evening, apparently while as high as a kite. Jessie couldn't help but think that if Vivien had uncovered his hypocrisy, it might make her very angry, even murderously so.

"How did you react to that?" she asked.

"What can I say? I was devastated," she admitted. "But I couldn't show him that. So I put on a brave face and acted like everything was cool; that it was all for the best. We kissed on the cheek and I left his room."

Jessie had a sudden recollection of the prior afternoon, out on the deck she was looking at now, when Valentine had asked Vivien if she and Eddie were close. Before the woman answered, she had taken a long pause to pour herself another drink. Was that simply a stalling tactic so that she could come up with a believable response?

Now that she thought about it, Jessie recalled something else too: while Joe Baldwin was happily singing along to Kenny Loggins, Vivien had been much less enthusiastic, barely speaking at all. Yes, she was drinking, but was that an act of celebration or a way of drowning her sorrows?

"What did you do once you left his suite?" Valentine asked Vivien, pulling Jessie back to the here and now.

"First I went back to our room and cried," she said. "Then I washed my face and started plotting my revenge."

"I'm sorry, what?" Jessie said.

Vivien must have realized how that sounded and quickly waved her hand as if she was erasing her words.

"I don't mean it like that," she said. "I came up with a plan while we were at dinner that night to blow the whole thing up. I decided that once the jet landed in L.A. the next morning, before everyone got off, I was going to out him—out us—and reveal our whole affair in front of everyone. I figured I'd make good on that whole mutually assured destruction thing. Both marriages would be ruined and then we could start our life together, fresh. Obviously I never got the chance to do that."

Jessie wasn't sure how much of this to believe but she quickly learned where Valentine stood.

"Are you sure about that?" the detective asked Vivien sharply.

"What do you mean?"

"We know about your background in the pharma industry," Valentine accused. "Someone like that might have access to large quantities of illegal substances, not to mention a lot of know-how about drug interactions."

After getting over her shock, Vivien half-laughed at the allegation.

"It's not like I was a research scientist or something, Detective," she countered, regaining some of the haughtiness that had defined her at the hangar yesterday. "I was an executive."

"But you majored in biochemistry," Valentine shot back.

"Sure, in college, years ago, back when I thought I wanted to be a doctor, before I decided that medical school and years of training was more than I was willing to sign up for. The degree was enough to get me in the door at the drug company. I could speak their language. But I was never involved in anything science-y after that."

"Maybe," Valentine acknowledged, "but that makes you a much stronger suspect than folks whose expertise is in selling music downloads."

Vivien chugged the last of her drink before replying.

"Listen, even if I wanted to poison Eddie and knew how to do it, I'm not sure how you think I realistically could have."

"Why not?" Valentine demanded.

"Didn't you hear what it was like on that plane?" Vivien challenged. "Music was blaring at full volume. Lights were flashing on and off. At one point there were even strobes. Everyone was drinking, doing drugs, and dancing half-naked in half-darkness. Even if I meant him harm, with everything going on, I was probably just as likely to drug the wrong person."

Valentine opened her mouth to challenge the point, but before she could get a word out, Vivien went on.

"Anyway, why would I admit to wanting any kind of revenge if I had actually drugged him? I may be a lush and half in the bag right now, but I'm not an idiot."

"That's awfully convenient," Valentine retorted, obviously put out that Vivien had cut her off. "Some might argue that admitting that you wanted revenge was just a pre-emptive move since you knew your affair would eventually come out and you'd look bad for hiding it."

"You give me too much credit," Vivien said dismissively.

"But you just said you're not an idiot," Valentine replied. "I'm just taking you at your word. Let's look at the facts, Mrs. Baldwin. You had an affair with Eddie Morse. He ended things definitively with you on Sunday night. Then he is poisoned on a Monday morning flight you shared with him. You have training in biochemistry and worked for a pharmaceutical company until just four years ago. Your phone data indicates that you are still in close contact with several people from that company. Eddie's death now puts your husband in charge of the company, with you by his side. What would you do in our shoes?"

"I'd stopping pointing fingers and do some real investigative work," Vivien argued.

Jessie wasn't enthused at how rapidly this had escalated. Valentine's aggression was unlikely to get a confession, assuming one was merited. In fact, at that very moment, Vivien Baldwin's expression was hardening. Any chance of getting her to admit culpability by sympathizing with her situation was out the door.

Whether the woman was guilty or not—and Jessie wasn't sure where she stood on that—taking this tack seemed like a terrible strategic choice. But Valentine was committed to it, and that meant that as her partner, Jessie had to be too. She knew what was coming next.

"How's this for some real investigative work?" Valentine barked, standing up. "Vivien Baldwin—you're under arrest for the murder of Edward Morse."

She pulled out a pair of handcuffs and proceeded to snap them on the stunned Vivien.

Jessie stood up too, groaning silently to herself. She had a bad feeling that Susannah Valentine had just shot their case to hell.

CHAPTER TWENTY EIGHT

Jessie felt like she was simultaneously watching and participating in a train wreck.

In the Central Station interrogation room, she mostly sat quietly as Valentine continued to press Vivien Baldwin to confess. She'd been at it for almost fifteen minutes, without success.

To Jessie's surprise, even after the detective read Vivien her rights, she didn't ask for a lawyer. Instead she continued to stubbornly assert her innocence. It was a battle of wills that no one was clearly winning.

"You can ask it as many different ways as you want, Detective," she insisted, the handcuffs attaching her to the metal table clanging as she gesticulated wildly, "but I'm not going to admit to something I didn't do. Working for a drug company isn't a crime. Having an affair isn't a crime in this country, at least not yet. Neither is being a bitch, or I'd have been thrown in jail a long time ago. And you would have too."

Jessie could see Valentine getting riled up again. She had tried to find a moment to talk to the detective privately before they started the questioning, but Valentine was so gung ho that she marched Vivien straight into the interrogation room and started hammering at her. Now Jessie decided to make another attempt.

"Detective Valentine," she said, trying not to betray any air of judgment, "maybe we should give Mrs. Baldwin a few minutes alone. Perhaps when we come back in, she'll have reconsidered how she wants to handle things."

She hoped that she came across as supportive, despite her reservations. Valentine looked over at her and it was clear that, while she was frustrated, she was happy to have an excuse to take a break.

"That sounds good," she agreed. "Let's see if a little time in this room with your thoughts and your cuffs will help clarify things for you."

Vivien started to respond but Jessie jumped in.

"Great," she said enthusiastically, standing up and guiding her partner out. "Everyone enjoy your private time. I know I could use a little break."

She closed the door before Vivien thought of a quippy comeback. Once in the hallway, she turned to Valentine.

"Let's get some fresh air. My favorite police station courtyard awaits."

Without waiting for a reply, she led the way to the door and held it open. Valentine reluctantly went through it. Though it was 2 p.m. and the height of the afternoon, it was overcast and there was a chill in the air. Jessie zipped up her jacket as she walked over to the bench in the middle of the courtyard and sat down. Valentine joined her but stayed standing.

Jessie was about to talk when her phone buzzed. She looked at the screen. It was a group text from Dr. Lemmon, sent to Hannah as well. From such a noted technophobe, that was an even rarer event than the call she received yesterday and caused the same anxious reaction. The message was simple: *I would like to speak with both of you today, in person. I am available in the day or evening. Let me know what works.*

The words were innocuous enough, but after dozens, if not hundreds of sessions with Janice Lemmon, Jessie knew this was something significant. The message had an unspoken tone of urgency. There was no point in guessing what it was. Lemmon would tell them directly when they met. She quickly texted back that she'd make it happen, tried to put it out of her head, and returned her attention to Valentine.

"So I think you'd agree that things aren't going super well in there," she said, nodding in the direction of the interrogation room.

"I'll admit that we've hit a snag," Valentine said. "But once she starts to comprehend the enormity of what she's facing, I think she'll start to weaken."

Jessie didn't want to be confrontational but she needed to get her point across. This case had gone sideways even before Valentine pulled out those cuffs and arrested Vivien Baldwin in her living room. It was time to get it back on track.

"I'm not so sure," she said as diplomatically as she could.

"What do you mean?" Valentine asked, her eyes narrowing.

"Vivien could easily be our killer," Jessie said, easing into her reservations. "The affair, the breakup, the pharma background, and the knowledge of biochemistry are all legitimate sources of suspicion. But I'm not convinced that proves she's guilty."

"Why not?"

"For one thing," she began. "She admitted to the affair. Now I know you think that was a pre-emptive move so she wouldn't look like she was keeping a secret. And that's possible. But it's also possible that the affair would have never come out if she'd said nothing. We didn't know about it. Apparently neither did their spouses. And the one other person who did know about it is dead. She could have stayed quiet and it might never have come to light."

"That's a big risk for her to take," Valentine said.

"Not if she doesn't think she did anything criminal," Jessie pointed out. "Telling us about the affair puts her marriage at risk regardless, but it only puts her freedom at risk if she's guilty. Just like answering hard-charging questions from a detective without her lawyer present only makes sense if she doesn't think she's done anything that will put her behind bars."

"Or she could just think she'll outsmart us," Valentine countered, "like Kurt Sumner, that murderous in-home chef, tried to do to you. He sat in an interrogation room with you forever, happy to play mental games with you, right up until the moment you turned the tables on him."

Jessie was surprised that Valentine even remembered the particulars of that case, which she'd only been tangentially involved in.

"Fair point," she acknowledged, "But I don't get the sense that Vivien is playing with us. Sumner relished getting us twisted up. She just keeps repeating that she's innocent, as if saying it often enough will convince us that it's true. But there's something else."

"What?" Valentine asked.

"There was no reason for her to kill Eddie," she said bluntly. "Remember, Vivien said they were always on-again, off-again. Based on their past experience, she had to assume that at some point, they'd be on-again. And she'd probably be right. If he hadn't died, I'd bet that despite what he said, Eddie would have been hooking up with her again within a week. We already know that he made a move on Bella the maid *the very same night*."

Valentine looked like she wanted to object but couldn't come up with a compelling argument. Jessie took advantage of her hesitation to keep going.

"I'm also not convinced that her science major and past pharma work make much difference with a crime like this. If someone was intent on killing Eddie this way, it wouldn't require a degree in the subject to make it happen. Just about anyone would know that a whole bag of heroin dumped in an alcoholic drink is going to do damage."

"Maybe, but with where she worked, she might have easier access to that quantity of it," Valentine pointed out.

"That could be," Jessie conceded. "But even so, I think she was right about something else too: considering how crazy it was on that jet,

133

with all the drugs and drinking and dancing, it sounds like the place was essentially a nightclub in the sky. How do we know that Eddie was even the intended victim? It was dark. It was loud. It was crowded. How can we be sure that Vivien, or anyone for that matter, didn't inadvertently slip the heroin into the wrong person's drink?"

As she said the words, she realized that Vivien's suggestion that it was too chaotic for her to be sure she was poisoning Eddie, even if she wanted to, wasn't just a credible defense. It actually made as much sense as the assumption that Eddie was the target of the poisoning. What if they'd been thinking about this all wrong? She looked over at Valentine, who had been watching her closely.

"It's obvious that you've had some kind of epiphany," the detective said. "Care to share?"

"I don't know anything for sure," Jessie said, trying to control her excitement. "But I think we need to strongly consider two alternative theories that we've largely dismissed: either Eddie was mistakenly drugged by someone with different prey in mind; or the killer was someone who could keep track of who had what drink at what time, specifically a professional at that kind of thing, like say, a flight attendant."

"You think it was one of them?" Valentine asked incredulously. "Did either of them even have a motive?"

"Not that we know of," Jessie conceded. "But we never really probed too hard. We focused our attention on the passengers, and with good reason. But I think it's an angle we probably should have explored further before arresting Vivien Baldwin."

She knew that last comment might rub her partner the wrong way. But she couldn't hold back on at least some level of criticism of the detective's premature desire to slap cuffs on Vivien Baldwin. To her credit, Valentine took it reasonably well. When she responded, she didn't sound defensive.

"I still think that Baldwin is the most likely culprit, considering what we know," she said evenly, "but maybe I was a little quick in bringing her in here. Still, I don't think we should just release her."

"We can hold her for a while longer," Jessie replied. "I'll tell her that we're investigating other avenues and that if they bear out, we'll release her quietly. I bet she'll agree to that just to keep her affair quiet. We can use that time to follow up on these other leads."

"Okay," Valentine agreed. "So where do you want to start?"

"I think we should have Jamil and Beth looking at the flight attendant logs. They can get a little more granular on the movements of both flight attendants. We know they kept digital logs on iPads of when they completed tasks like food service, lavatory checks, etc. They just had to check off each item once it was done. But until now, we didn't really have cause to study the logs closely. While they do that, you and I can split up and go visit each of them separately to save time. If Jamil and Beth find anything while we're en route, they can let us know. Sound cool?"

Valentine must have thought it was because she was already headed for the courtyard door.

CHAPTER TWENTY NINE

Jessie made good time.

As she pulled up across the street from Anna De Luca's apartment building, she looked at the time. It was 2:36 p.m. Less than twenty minutes ago, she'd been in the research department with Valentine, Jamil, and Beth.

"I managed to convince Vivien that waiting in that interrogation room was her best bet to get out of all this without ruining her life," she had told the others. "But if we take too long, I'm worried that, despite the risk to her reputation, she'll call a lawyer and everything will get mucked up."

Valentine, who was clearly not enthused by the idea of Vivien Baldwin bringing an attorney into the process, didn't need to be told to get going. She left without another word, headed straight for the parking garage and then on to DeDe Albright's place.

That left Jessie to visit Anna De Luca, who lived on North Rossmore Avenue, a busy Hancock Park street just south of Hollywood. As she got out of the car, she glanced up the block and saw a familiar sight. Only a few hundred yards away was the Beverly Country Club.

That was the place where she'd first met Andy Robinson while investigating the murder of another member of the club. Of course, Andy had turned out to be the killer she was looking for. But initially she had come across as a surprisingly self-effacing socialite who was happy to give a fresh-faced profiler working her first case the inside scoop on the social politics of the club.

Jessie laughed bitterly at the realization that circumstances hadn't changed all that much. Even after all the intervening cases since then, she was still somehow intertwined with Andy. Only now, instead of getting the gossip on country club members, she was trading cushier prison hospital conditions for the chance at getting the inside scoop on mentally unstable patients who might have ill intent and the means to act on it.

All this sordid nostalgia about Andy Robinson reminded Jessie that Andy's transfer was scheduled for two days ago and that she really ought to check in to make sure the woman hadn't caused any trouble since being moved. Maybe after all this was over.

As she walked toward Anna De Luca's building, she called Jamil.

"Have you got anything for me?" she asked.

"Hold on," he said. "I'm handing you off to Beth. I think she might."

A second later the young researcher picked up. Jessie knew immediately that she'd made a discovery.

"Hi, Jessie," she said excitedly. "I noticed something odd in De Luca's log."

"Tell me."

"Well, normally, I'd dismiss it but considering the circumstances, I thought it unusual."

"I'm walking up to her building right now, Beth," Jessie said, fighting to keep her impatience in check. "So just give it to me straight."

"Okay, sorry. There's a fifteen minute gap in her log, where she doesn't seem to have been doing any flight attendant duties. Like I said, normally it wouldn't seem so weird for there to be a lull like that. But on this flight, with these passengers, down time seems like a luxury they didn't have. And other than that one stretch of time, she's crazy busy. Not more than six minutes goes by during the rest of the flight without her registering some task begun or completed."

"When was she out of commission?" Jessie asked.

"From 9:37 to 9:52."

"That's well before DeDe Albright discovered Eddie dead."

"Correct," Beth said. "Albright found him at about 10:15."

Jessie was about to respond when she saw a familiar face coming out of Anna De Luca's building: Gareth Thacker.

"Okay, thanks Beth," she said hurriedly. "That's great work. I've got to go."

She hung up quickly as the swarthy record producer walked down the path from the building to the sidewalk. In addition to his seemingly standard out-of-control blond hair and bloodshot eyes, he also had a leer plastered across his chubby, stubbly face.

"Fancy meeting you here, Jessie," he said, popping hard on her first name, clearly hoping to annoy her with his inappropriate familiarity.

"Awfully coincidental," she replied, doing her best to hide both her surprise at his presence and her annoyance at his verbal tweak. "I know you don't live here. Who are you visiting?"

She allowed herself a moment of anticipation, hoping that he might lie. That would give her reason to further question the guy who, despite everything she'd learned about Eddie Morse, still held the title as most repugnant passenger on the jet.

"I think you probably already know, Jessie," he told her smarmily. I was visiting Anna D, just as I imagine you're about to."

"Anna D?"

"Yeah," he said. "I'm playing with that as a stage name for her."

Jessie couldn't hide her surprise at that.

"Do you really expect me to believe that you're here for professional reasons?"

Thacker came as close to looking offended as she thought was possible for him.

"Don't get me wrong," he said. "Under normal circumstances, I'd tap that in a second. The girl's a credible hottie. But I genuinely don't like to mix business and pleasure until I'm comfortable that the business part is going smoothly."

"What does that mean?"

"Just that I wanted to make sure that she's either a bust or a hit, talent-wise, before I try to take advantage of her."

"And which is she?" Jessie wondered, still skeptical of every word he was saying.

"She's got talent," he said sincerely, holding up his phone. "I've got multiple recordings of her singing in a variety of styles—upbeat pop, ballads, a little R&B. She nailed all of them. Her voice is golden. If she's got the work ethic to go with it, she might have a chance. And with everything so unsettled at Eddie Records, I could use a new 'it girl' in my stable."

"How did you even find out that she could sing?" Jessie asked suspiciously. "Did she just start belting something out for you on the jet?"

Thacker smiled devilishly.

"That's not my place to say," he told her. "You'll have to ask her yourself when you go up there. Speaking of which, why is she getting a second interview and not me? Should I be hurt?"

He pretended to pout.

"The day's not over, Gareth," she replied, popping his first name as he had with her.

"Don't tease me, Jessie Hunt," he parried. "I'm happy to oblige you—maybe at my place, this evening, over a bottle of Shiraz or three?"

"I'll let you know," she told him, impressively holding back the sudden desire to throw up in her mouth.

"I'll wait anxiously by the phone, future love," he cooed, before turning and walking off. He clearly didn't expect a reply.

Once he left, Jessie returned her attention to the job at hand. But now, in addition to trying to determine if Anna De Luca was a killer, she was also curious to know how the woman might suddenly be on the verge of becoming a pop starlet named Anna D.

If she was, she'd picked the right place to start that journey. This stretch of Rossmore, just south of where it hit Hollywood and became Vine Street, was lined with old-school apartment complexes that looked like they were right of a 1940s noir film. There was the legendary El Royale, along with The Hermoyne, and the Ravenswood, where screen stars like Mae West, Clark Gable, and Ava Gardner all lived for a time.

Anna lived at The Sullivan, which had the same glamorous look on the outside, complete with art deco design and palm trees out front. But when she walked into the lobby, it was a different matter. The place smelled stale and visible dust rose up off the boysenberry-colored carpet with every step. Anna lived on the fourth floor and even though there was a treacherous-looking elevator, Jessie took the stairs.

Once she got to unit 408, she undid her gun holster as a precaution. After all, Anna De Luca might be a killer. If she was, there was no telling what she might do if cornered. Jessie knocked without verbally announcing herself, curious about the response she'd get. The door opened seconds later.

"Did you forget somethi—?" De Luca began before stopping suddenly when she saw who her guest was.

"Hi, Anna. How's it going?" Jessie asked pleasantly, as if her arrival had been expected.

"Okay," the young woman responded hesitantly.

Out of her flight attendant uniform and wearing pop-star style attire, Thacker was right. She was a credible hottie. Unlike yesterday when it was pulled back in a bun, her blonde hair caressed her shoulders, which were exposed by her gray, *Flashdance*-style sweater. She had on pink, form-fitting pants, which accentuated her curves. She was wearing more makeup too, as if she was about to head out to a club for the night.

"Mind if I come in?" Jessie wondered. "I have a few more questions about the flight yesterday."

"I guess," Anna said, opening the door reluctantly. "Did I do something wrong?"

"I don't know, Anna," Jessie asked as she walked inside. "Did you?"

Anna closed the door without responding and led the way to the couch, which wasn't much of a walk. As it turned out, the place was essentially a large studio apartment with a nook for the bed. The unit was spartan, with just the couch, two chairs at a small table, the bed, and a small chest of drawers. Apparently she wasn't getting rich off the flight attendant game.

"Are you talking about Gareth Thacker?" she asked as they sat down. "I'm assuming you saw him on your way up here."

"We spoke," Jessie acknowledged. "He said you're very talented. I guess I'm just wondering why it took until yesterday for anyone to notice."

"It's not what you think," Anna said defensively. "I didn't sleep with him."

"I didn't say you did," Jessie countered, holding her palms up in surrender, though that was exactly what she was thinking.

"All I did was take advantage of an opportunity," Anna insisted. "I tried to break into music for years when I first got to L.A. No one gave me a real chance. Every guy made a move on me. It was so depressing that after a while, I just gave up. That's when I became a flight attendant. But Gareth heard me singing on the flight yesterday and thought I sounded good so he offered to follow up today. I was sure he was just saying that to get in my pants."

"But he wasn't?" Jessie wanted to know.

"I'm not saying he won't try at some point. He was hitting on DeDe pretty hard on the jet yesterday. But for now at least, he was professional."

Jessie recalled DeDe mentioning that Anna had rescued her from a potentially scary situation.

"Okay, Anna," she said, trying to hide her skepticism that her lucky break had played out as described. "I hope that all works out for you. In the meantime, since you mentioned the jet, I wanted to ask you something about the flight."

Okay," she replied, looking nervous, but not "am I about to be busted for murder?" nervous. Jessie decided to test that out by cutting straight to the chase.

"How many drinks did you serve Eddie Morse during the flight?"

Anna seemed relieved at the question.

"None," she said definitively.

"How is that possible? I heard he was drinking the whole flight."

"He was. But he had his own bottle. He opened it as soon he got onboard and just kept filling up his glass over and over again. I offered to serve him but he said that he was happy being his own bartender. He was more than two-thirds of the way through it when he…you know."

That description fit with what DeDe had told her yesterday about Eddie preferring to lubricate himself. She decided to veer sharply in another direction.

"Right," she said. "Hey Anna, can you tell me what you were doing on the jet from 9:27 to 9:52?"

"Huh?" the girl said, her face immediately turning beet red.

"Your digital log from the flight indicates that you didn't register any tasks during that stretch. I'm just wondering what you were doing then."

"What does that have to do with anything?" Anna asked defensively.

"Just answer the question please."

Anna looked back at her silently and Jessie watched an array of emotions pass across her face in mere seconds. She lowered her head. Jessie, unsure what was coming, eased her hand closer to her holster. When Anna looked up again, her eyes were rimmed with tears.

"I wasn't totally honest before," she said heavily.

"About what?" Jessie asked, wondering if she was about to get a confession.

"I told you that Gareth heard me singing on the jet and that's what got him interested in coming over today. But it wasn't Gareth who first heard me. It was Glenn Ward."

"The doctor?" Jessie confirmed.

"Right," Anna replied. "I was prepping some food in the galley, singing to myself, when he came in to get a chocolate éclair. He told me that I had a really good voice and that he could try to set up a recording session with Gareth. But he said that in order to put himself on the line like that, he needed to hear me sing under better circumstances. He suggested the rear lavatory might be good 'because of the acoustics.'"

"I see," Jessie said quietly.

The tears were now trickling down Anna's cheeks.

"It's hard to explain exactly why I did it," she said hoarsely. "I think that in that moment I just kind of cracked. I was so tired of working crazy hours for impossible people and getting paid peanuts. I mean, look at this place. It's embarrassing. I had this flash of a different life that might be possible. I was only feet away from a major record producer *and* a guy who owned a music label. I thought that if this doctor was tight enough to be partying on a jet with them, maybe he really could hook me up. So I decided to take a chance."

"And you met him in the lavatory?"

"Yeah," she whispered. "I guess it could have been worse. I kept my eyes closed most of the time and he was so messed up on whatever he'd taken that he could barely do the deed. Then it was over and we left."

"Did anyone see you exiting the bathroom?"

Anna thought about it for a moment.

"Actually, yes," she said. "Eddie was waiting outside to use it."

"This would have been around 9:50 a.m., about twenty five minutes before DeDe discovered him dead?"

"That sounds right," she confirmed.

"How did he look?" Jessie asked.

"Fine, I guess. I mean, he was clearly drunk or high or both. But he was functional. He did look a little pissed though."

"At you?" Jessie pressed.

"No," she answered. "At Dr. Ward. He kind of glowered at him as we walked past him. Glenn looked pretty sheepish."

"Did Eddie say why he might be angry?"

"Nuh-uh," she said. "I just assumed that he was annoyed that he had to wait to use the bathroom. Maybe the front lavatory was occupied."

Jessie had another theory; one that she kept to herself. Yes, maybe Eddie was just anxious to pee. Or perhaps he saw that one of his friends had created a liability issue by hooking up with someone who worked for the aviation company. If she claimed she was assaulted on a jet that was owned by the Qatari venture capital firm that had bailed out his company, it could have devastating effects.

Or maybe Eddie was just pissed that Ward had cheated on his wife, Lucy, with whom he'd been friends since their freshman year of college. Just because Eddie was an adulterous bastard in his own right didn't mean he was cool with one of his friends betraying another one.

Whatever the reason, Jessie realized that one of her suspects had just risen in prominence. Dr. Glenn Ward knew that Eddie was pissed at him. And if Eddie's anger was about something more than having to wait for the bathroom, be it Glenn's infidelity or putting his business at risk of legal liability, Ward might have panicked.

The fear that must have consumed him as he pondered what Edward Morse might do. What if Eddie cut him off completely because he viewed him as a millstone? Or what if he told Lucy about her husband's visit to the mile high club? In his diminished cognitive state, might Glenn Ward have taken drastic measures to hide his secret liaison? As a doctor, he would have known better than anyone what a massive dose of heroin mixed in with alcohol would do to Eddie's system.

"Ms. Hunt?" Anna said softly.

Jessie blinked. The girl was looking at her nervously, not sure why her interrogator had gone silent for ten seconds.

"Sorry," she said. "I was just playing something out in my head."

"So am I in trouble?" Anna asked, wiping the tears from her cheek.

Jessie couldn't dismiss the possibility that the flight attendant was the killer. But the more she thought about it, the less likely it seemed. Right now, there was no point in bringing her in or even revealing that Eddie had been murdered.

"Not from me, at least not yet," she said. "But you might be putting *yourself* in trouble. I'm not here to judge your choices. But you'd do well to be careful. I know Gareth Thacker is a talented, big-time producer, but he's also a lecherous scumbag. If it was me, I wouldn't be too accommodating. He knows you've got talent now, and after Eddie's death, his professional world is on shaky ground too. He might not want to risk losing you as a potential cash cow just to get you into bed. Use that to your advantage."

That got a hint of a smile from Anna.

"Thanks," she said.

"Sure," Jessie replied, before adding, "and by the way, I wouldn't leave town. Until this case is closed, it could look bad."

As soon as she left the apartment, she called Valentine. It went straight to voicemail so she texted for her to call her right back. When she didn't get a response by the time she got to her car, she called Jamil instead. Beth picked up.

"Hey," Jessie said, "I need you to find out if Dr. Glenn Ward is at his home or his office right now, and then send me the address for his current location. And please get in touch with Valentine and tell her to meet me there. Her phone is going straight to voicemail and I can't keep calling and texting. Then I want you to check up on Ward: his specialty, his financial situation, if his wife ever filed for separation, anything that seems off. Can you do all that?"

"We'll split it up," Beth said.

"Thanks," Jessie said. "And please hurry on that address. I want to make a house call on this guy ASAP."

CHAPTER THIRTY

She didn't have to go far.

Just minutes after hanging up, she got a text from Beth saying that Glenn Ward was at home, which just so happened to be in the same Hancock Park neighborhood that Anna lived in, albeit in a fancier area dominated by large mansions.

Five minutes later, just after 3.p.m, she pulled up across the street and waited for Valentine to arrive so they could question the doctor together. The detective was coming from DeDe Albright's apartment in West Hollywood and it would take her another ten minutes to get here.

While she settled in to wait, Jessie took in the impressive Ward home. It was a large, Tudor style mansion with a manicured front lawn, complete with a topiary garden that probably cost more to regularly maintain than Anna De Luca's salary.

Jessie acidly noted that this was the same neighborhood that Andy Robinson used to live in before she got busted. In fact, her former mansion, where she'd poisoned Jessie during that girls' movie night gone bad, was just two streets over. The memory of it still smarted, less so for the brush with death than her embarrassing naïveté on that first case, when it never really occurred to her to be suspicious of Andy. It was a hard way to learn the lesson.

The thought reminded Jessie that she needed to check in with the PDC to make sure Andy's transfer had gone without incident. She dialed the private office number for the facility administrator, Maggie Conrad, who picked up on the second ring.

"PDC, Conrad here," she said simply.

"Hi Ms. Conrad, it's Jessie Hunt. I was just checking in on Andrea Robinson. How's she doing there so far? Any issues with her transfer or subsequently?"

"Hello, Ms. Hunt," Conrad replied. "I know you wanted a close eye kept on Ms. Robinson. But at least to this point, there haven't been any issues. Her transition has gone smoothly. She hasn't made any trouble. We monitored her first daily phone call, which went without incident."

"Who did she call?"

"One of her therapists back at Twin Towers—she thanked her for treating her, bland stuff."

"And has she started sessions with you guys yet?"

"She had her first one yesterday," Conrad told her. "Obviously I'm not privy to the content of that conversation and couldn't share it with you unless the psychiatrist determined that she was an imminent threat to herself or others, but generally speaking, my understanding is that it went well."

Jessie had more questions but Beth was buzzing in, so she cut it short.

"I have another call," she said quickly, "but I'd like to check in regularly with you if that's all right?"

"Of course, Ms. Hunt—any time."

Jessie switched over.

"What's up, Beth?"

"I just wanted to fill you in on what I found out about Glenn Ward."

"Go for it."

"According to the records, he's a general practitioner, kind of a concierge doctor. He only has about a dozen patients, all wealthy. Most of them have some personal or professional affiliation with Eddie Morse, which may be how he got them."

"That might explain why he might have gotten concerned if Morse got mad at him," Jessie noted. "It sounds like Eddie was his golden goose. If he cut him off or spoke ill of him, Ward's patient list might dry up pretty fast. Any legal issues—malpractice lawsuits in his past?"

"Nothing that I could find," Beth said. "And no indication of any separation papers either. They have one child, a daughter. Family life seems solid. The only thing I noticed was an unusual uptick in cash withdrawals in the last month. I can't find any corresponding purchases."

"What kind of withdrawals are we talking about," Jessie asked suspiciously.

"In the first week, it was around $1500. They've gone up gradually since then. On the morning that they left L.A. to go up north, he took out $7000. What do you think it's for?"

"Hard to know for sure," Jessie said, though she had an idea. "I will say that those kinds of increasing withdrawals sometimes suggest an escalating drug habit. It makes me wonder if he might have been buying large quantities of something, maybe heroin."

"Well, I guess you're about to get the chance to find out. He's waiting for you as we speak."

Jessie felt a cold shiver of alarm shoot up her spine.

"Wait, did you tell him we were coming?" she asked.

146

"Yes," Beth said, clearly sensing that she'd done something wrong. "When his office said he left early to take some personal time, I called the house to make sure he was there. Should I not have?"

Before Jessie could respond, she heard Jamil's voice, much louder than usual, in the background.

"No, you shouldn't have," he said forcefully. "Now he knows the police are coming. He could dispose of evidence, make a run for it, or get a weapon."

"I didn't think—," a shaken Beth started to say before Jessie cut her off.

"What exactly did he say?"

"I didn't talk to him," Beth said. "Lucy Ward picked up. When I told her you'd be coming by, she said that she'd let him know. I'm so sorry. Now it's obvious to me that it was a mistake."

"Right now, let's just focus on fixing it," Jessie told her, trying to keep her frustration in check. "I can't wait for Valentine anymore. Who knows what Ward is doing in there, possibly to his wife. I'm going in. Call Valentine back and tell her to double time it. And send a couple of black and whites too. Got it?"

"Yes, ma'am," Beth said hurriedly, no longer using the first name.

Jessie got out of the car and was just darting across the street to the Ward mansion when the front door opened. Standing on the porch, looking stricken, was Lucy Ward. She was wearing yoga pants and a sleeveless top and looked like she'd just been in the middle of a workout. When she saw Jessie, she waved wildly at her.

"I need help," she yelled. "I think Glenn's in trouble."

Jessie broke into a run.

"What happened?" she demanded when she got closer. Lucy Ward hurriedly ushered her in.

"When I told him you'd be coming by," she said as she scampered down the hallway with Jessie right behind her, "he said he had to do something in his office. But when I checked on him just now after I finished my workout, the door was locked and he wouldn't respond. I'm worried that something's terribly wrong."

They reached his office door and Jessie tried opening it. It was indeed locked.

"Dr. Ward," she called out. "This is Jessie Hunt. Are you okay in there?"

There was no reply.

"Dr. Ward," she went on. "Your wife is concerned about you. If you don't answer, I'm going to have to break down the door. Please respond."

Still nothing.

"Stand back," she instructed Lucy, who looked on the verge of losing it entirely. The woman took a few steps back. Jessie unholstered her weapon, unsure what was waiting for her in that room, then stepped forward and kicked the door near the handle. The door cracked near the jamb but didn't open. She repeated the maneuver. This time it flew open.

At first she didn't see anything. But then she caught sight of Ward near his desk, lying on the floor beside the desk chair. She quickly moved over and saw that he was unconscious. He was breathing, but just barely. She pulled out her phone and dialed the dedicated number for law enforcement emergencies. Once she gave the EMT dispatcher the address and situation, she got down on her knees, put her phone and gun down beside her, and began CPR.

"Did he say anything else?" she demanded of his wife while doing chest compressions.

"Um," Lucy said, wracking her brain. "He mentioned something about making a terrible mistake and needing to correct it. I thought he'd forgotten to prescribe a patient a medication or something. Is he going to be okay?"

"Had he been acting differently lately?" Jessie asked, ignoring the question as she pressed on the man's chest. Her breathing was getting labored and she could already feel her arms started to tire. Lucy Ward didn't answer at first and it was clear that he had been.

"This is no time to hold back, Lucy. Tell me."

The woman seemed to break at that.

"He has been different," she conceded. "It started when he snorted heroin for the first time about a month ago. He hid it from me but when I noticed money missing from our account, I confronted him. He admitted to it and said he'd stop. But then I saw more money disappear and I knew he was still using. I told him he had to get help. He promised that he would, right after this trip."

"Okay, listen," Jessie instructed as sweat started to drip off her. "I need you to take over compressions for a minute so I can regain my strength. Can you do that?"

"Yeah," Lucy said, now starting to lose it as tears streamed down her face. "I learned child CPR a few years ago after Birdie was born. Thank God she's at my parents right now."

"It's the same concept," Jessie assured her, "just use the heels of your palms and apply more force, okay?"

Lucy nodded and got down on her knees.

"Okay," Jessie said. "Switch with me on my mark—now!"

She moved aside and Lucy slid in and began compressions. Jessie allowed herself a few seconds to regroup. She stood up and took several, long deep breaths. Her arms and chest were burning.

On Glenn Ward's desk, beside a large, glass paperweight inscribed with the phrase "Doc of the walk," she noticed a mostly empty glass tumbler with a little white residue inside. She could guess what it was. Maybe the man had decided that it would be poetic justice to take himself out the same way he'd eliminated his friend.

"I'm going to check on the status of the ambulance," she said once she'd mostly caught her breath. Looking at Lucy pushing on her husband's chest, she added, "just keep doing what you're doing."

She reached down for her phone, which she'd placed on the floor when she first started compressions. As she grabbed it, she noticed that her gun was missing. She bent down and saw that it was well under Glenn's desk, where it must have been inadvertently kicked in all the commotion. She couldn't worry about grabbing it right now. Instead, she dialed the emergency number again. She noticed that her fingers were shaking because of adrenaline and the effort she'd expended doing CPR. As she called, she observed that Lucy was no longer pushing anywhere near hard enough.

"You need to put more weight behind it," she told her as she waited for the call to connect. "I know you don't want to hurt him but better to break a rib than not use enough force."

Lucy nodded. Jessie was a little surprised. The woman's arms were rippled with muscles and according to Vivien Baldwin's outburst yesterday, she was a CrossFit fiend. Even under duress, she should have more endurance than this. The call connected.

"What's the status on my emergency vehicle?" she wanted to know.

"Three minutes out," the dispatcher said.

"Tell them to have the Narcan ready. I think we've got a heroin overdose here."

She hung up and returned her attention to Lucy and Glenn. Once again, she saw that the woman wasn't applying enough pressure.

"Let me take over again," she said. Lucy moved and she took her place.

She could immediately tell that she wasn't going to last much longer. Her shoulders felt wobbly and her forearms were on fire. She

149

tried to ignore the pain and clear her head, focusing all her attention on maintaining the rhythm of the compressions. It only took a few seconds for her to get the cadence.

As her mind emptied, filled only with the desire to keep this man alive until the EMTs arrived, an unexpected thought popped into her head. She didn't remember accidentally knocking her gun under the desk. And Lucy hadn't done it when they changed spots. So how did it get there? It was so far under the desk that it seemed almost...intentional.

Though her body was exhausted, her brain got a renewed shot of adrenaline as the pieces fell into place. Her gun had been moved when she wasn't looking. Lucy, a workout fanatic, seemed unable, or uninterested in, giving maximum effort in order to keep her husband alive.

That's when it occurred to her that maybe Lucy didn't want him alive. Maybe Eddie Morse wasn't the only one who saw Glenn leave that jet lavatory with Anna De Luca. Maybe that sight, combined with the knowledge that her husband was now a full-on heroin addict, caused Lucy to snap and take drastic action using the very drug that was destroying their lives.

Maybe, with the private jet a chaotic jumble of flashing lights in darkness, pounding music, naked dancing, and people crowded tightly together, she had found her husband's stash of heroin and dumped the whole baggie of uncut powder into the wrong glass. After all, Eddie was in the bathroom, so she wouldn't have known that the tumbler resting unclaimed on the table was his and not Glenn's.

Jessie looked over at Lucy and saw that the woman was staring back at her through narrowed eyes. In that moment Jessie knew two things: First, that she was staring into the eyes of a murderer; and two, the murderer knew she'd been found out.

Before Jessie could even lift her hands off Glenn's chest, Lucy leapt at her.

CHAPTER THIRTY ONE

The woman knocked Jessie off of Glenn, slamming her into the side of his desk. Air shot out of her chest as she bounced off it and ended up flat on her back. As she was gasping for more air, Lucy pounced on top of her, pinning her down and wrapping her arms around her neck, making it infinitely harder to breathe.

Coherent thought fled her brain. She wanted to lash out but her arms were still weak and burning from all the compressions she'd done. Her eyes started to water. She tried to wriggle free but Lucy was amazingly strong. It felt like her head might pop off her neck at any moment.

Do something!

The voice in her head cut through all the pain and fear, and in that moment, she had a clear vision of what she had to do. With the palm of her right hand, the same one she'd just been using on Glenn's chest, she lashed out, smashing it hard into Lucy's windpipe.

The woman let go as she reached for her throat and began coughing uncontrollably. Jessie swung her palm up a second time, this time aiming higher. She made contact with Lucy's nose and heard a loud yelp.

As she sucked in air, Jessie pushed the other woman away, sending her tumbling off her. Then she rolled onto her stomach and started to crawl toward the broken office door. She'd only gotten a few feet when she felt hands grab her left ankle and yank her back. She twisted around to see Lucy, still coughing and with blood leaking from her nose. The woman was pulling her in like she was the rope in a game of tug of war. Her eyes were glowing with intensity and her lips had twisted into a nasty grimace.

Calling on what energy she had left, Jessie reared back with her right leg and kicked Lucy, sending her toppling backward. Then she turned around and resumed crawling. Her arms, simultaneously heavy and on fire, were only somewhat responsive.

She heard a wild scream behind her and glanced back. Lucy had recovered from the kick and gotten to her feet. In her right hand was Glenn's huge, glass "Doc of the walk" paperweight. She marched quickly toward Jessie, with the paperweight lifted high above her head.

151

Jessie rolled onto her butt and tried to push herself upright into a seated position to defend herself. But breathing was still difficult and her arms simply wouldn't do what she commanded. She realized she wouldn't be able to ward off Lucy's blow with her hands and, since the woman was coming at her from an angle, it was impossible to kick her again. She was a sitting duck.

This is it.

Lucy started to swing the paperweight down toward Jessie's head when a loud bang reverberated through the room. Almost concurrently, Lucy wailed in pain as she dropped the paperweight and tumbled forward past Jessie, missing her entirely as she collapsed head-first to the ground.

Confused, Jessie turned around to find Susannah Valentine standing in the office doorway. Her gun was pointed at Lucy, who was howling as she clutched her outer left thigh just above the knee. Jessie wanted to speak but found that she still couldn't catch her breath. Besides, her throat hurt too much. All she could muster was a shudder of relief.

"You okay?" the detective asked as she holstered her gun, pulled out her handcuffs, and moved over to Lucy Ward.

Jessie nodded weakly. Valentine cuffed Lucy, ignoring the woman's screams as she loudly read her rights. In between the caterwauling, Jessie could hear the distinct sound of sirens getting close. She looked over at Glenn Ward, who was still lying motionless on the floor by his desk. Valentine, focused on the woman in front of her, didn't seem to have noticed him.

Though it caused intense discomfort, Jessie managed to swallow hard before grunting, "Husband poisoned. Needs CPR."

When Valentine looked up, Jessie motioned in his direction with her head. The detective saw him but seemed torn between going to him and staying with the suspect, who was bleeding profusely from her leg.

"Help him," Jessie mumbled. "I got her."

"Okay," Valentine said as she scrambled over to the unconscious man. As she started compressions, Jessie looked around the office. Her eyes fell on an Oberlin College sweatshirt pinned to the wall near the door. She stumbled over to it, tore it off the wall, and dropped down next to Lucy.

The woman had gone from screeching to a low whimper. That was about to change. Jessie rolled her over onto her back and wrapped the sweatshirt around her thigh. Then she tied it off securely, leading to another round of yowls. She ignored it, as well as the blood seeping through the shirt onto her hands as she kept pressure on it.

"He stopped breathing!" Valentine shouted from across the room.

Lucy Ward stopped screeching long enough to smile at that news. The blood from her smashed nose had dripped down into her teeth, giving her a ghastly, zombie-like look.

"Keep at it," Jessie croaked, "EMTs almost here."

Just as she said it, two techs burst into the room, carrying a stretcher and supplies. They took stock of the situation. Jessie decided to help them.

"Him first," she said, nodding at Glenn. "Heroin OD. Not breathing. Needs Narcan."

The EMTs dashed over to Valentine. The male tech took over compressions while the female one prepared the Narcan injection.

"How long ago did he stop breathing?" she asked Valentine.

"Less than thirty seconds ago."

The tech administered the shot.

"How long will it take to work?" Valentine wanted to know.

"Usually two to three minutes," she said.

"Just let the bastard die," Lucy yelled across the room at them. "He deserves it."

That got the attention of Valentine, who came over and knelt down beside the woman who was lying on her back, trying not to wince.

"It seems like you've lost that loving feeling, Lucy," she said. "Is that why you poisoned him, just like you did to Eddie?"

Lucy half-chuckled, which led immediately to a pained groan. Once that subsided, she asked a question of her own.

"Are you—the woman who just shot me—really trying to get a confession out of me while I bleed to death?" she asked.

"If you're going to die, what difference does it make?" Valentine shot back.

Jessie was confident that, despite the blood, Lucy would pull through. The wound wasn't near any major arteries. And she could tell that Valentine suspected the same. The comment was just a tactic. Deciding she should employ one of her own, Jessie swallowed again and pushed through the soreness in her throat to speak.

"We already know you're guilty, Lucy," she said hoarsely, noting Valentine surreptitiously pull out her phone and hit record. "You basically just confessed now with your death wish declaration. There were four witnesses to it. And even if you hadn't said anything, you'd be toast. After all, why try to kill me if you're innocent? You knew I knew. You're going down for this, Lucy. The best you can hope for is to get a lighter sentence by justifying your actions."

153

She stopped to regroup. Her throat felt raw and she needed to swallow repeatedly to lubricate it enough to talk. Before she could continue, another pair of EMTs rushed into the room. Valentine pointed at Lucy.

"GSW to the exterior thigh," she said, "I tried to avoid any major arteries when I shot her."

"Her nose might be broken too," Jessie muttered, nodding at the swollen thing.

The EMTs nodded and moved in to look at the wounds. Jessie happily released her grip on the woman's bloody leg.

"By the way," Valentine continued, "do you guys have any numbing spray for my partner's throat? Based on the marks on her neck, I'm guessing your patient here tried to choke her to death."

One of the EMTs reached into his kit and tossed a spray to Jessie, who used it right away. Within seconds, she felt some of the sting start to subside. She was just about to test out her voice again when the female EMT beside Glenn Ward called out.

"He's breathing! Let's get him to the hospital."

"Dammit," Lucy muttered under her breath.

The EMTs moved him onto the stretcher and then quickly out the door. As the other two worked on Lucy, so did Jessie.

"Now we'll have a witness to how this all went down," she told her, finally able to speak in complete sentences without cringing. "You'd do well to get your story out there before he does."

"What story is going to change anything?" Lucy spat.

"I don't know," Jessie said before volunteering one. "Maybe the story that your husband had sunk into heroin addiction, was draining your bank accounts, wouldn't get help, and was putting your family at risk?"

"All that's true," Lucy said, surprised, "Just like I told you before."

"Yes, but you didn't tell me what pushed you over the edge," Jessie reminded her, before deciding to take a calculated risk. "Was it seeing him come out of the jet bathroom with that flight attendant?"

Lucy's mouth dropped open in shock. In that moment, Jessie knew that her theory was correct, even if she couldn't yet prove it. Now she just had to get the woman to admit to it.

"How did you know that?" she whispered.

"I know a lot more than you think," Jessie said, though these were just educated guesses. "I'm assuming she wasn't the first time he cheated on you."

Lucy shook her head.

154

"No," she said bitterly, "I found out that he'd been sleeping with one of his nurses for months. I threatened to leave him, so he broke it off, swore he'd never do it again. The heroin started a few weeks later. He admitted to that after I found out about all the cash withdrawals."

"This was his first time using?" Valentine confirmed. "I thought that you guys all liked to party pretty hard."

"We do...we did," Lucy acknowledged. "But that was just booze, weed, coke, maybe some Molly. We'd use it recreationally but it didn't affect our day to day. This was different. It grabbed him and didn't let go."

"He told you that?" Jessie asked.

"Kind of—he told me he tried it at a party and liked it too much. I'm sure that was true but I suspected that he might just be replacing a sex addiction with a drug addiction. That's why I stuck it out. I thought that if he went to rehab, we could get past it."

"But then you saw him with the flight attendant," Jessie prompted.

Lucy hung her head at the memory. At that very moment, one of the EMTs started to open his mouth. Jessie sensed that he was about to say they had to take her to the hospital. Valentine must have had the same thought because she immediately put her finger to her lips and shook her head as she glowered at the poor guy. He closed his mouth just before Lucy looked up again.

"Yes," she admitted quietly. "When I saw the two of them come out of that bathroom, it gutted me. I realized that I'd been deluding myself. He didn't replace cheating with heroin. He was making time for both."

"He didn't know that you saw him?" Valentine asked.

"No. Eddie was right outside the door waiting to use the bathroom and Glenn was focused on him and the girl. I darted behind the curtain. He never saw me. But I saw him give her one last furtive kiss. That's when I knew."

"Knew what?" Jessie pressed.

"I knew that there was no hope—that he would never change. And I guess I just kind of lost it."

"What do you mean?" Jessie asked quietly.

"I saw a future where he destroyed our lives—mine and Birdie's. I had this vision of him eventually switching to needles, shooting up with our daughter in the room. I pictured her coming across a used syringe and picking it up. And I knew he'd bleed us dry. My family is very well off. He would have drained our accounts completely. And if I divorced him, I risked losing my nest egg. My mind kept flashing between images of my family in ruin and Glenn and that stewardess whore going at it on a toilet. I snapped."

"So you decided to get poetic justice," Jessie cajoled, "by finishing him off with the very drug that was finishing your family off, right?"

Lucy nodded. She no longer seemed surprised that the profiler had seemingly read her mind. Valentine, on the other hand, looked astounded.

"I was pretty wasted and in that moment, it seemed perfect," Lucy admitted. "So I went to his carry-on and found his baggie of the stuff. He had told me it was pure, uncut, no impurities—that he had to be careful because it was so potent. So I dumped the whole baggie in his drink, or what I thought was his drink, and I mixed it around until you couldn't see the powder. No one was paying any attention to me. Everyone was watching Gareth do naked versions of dance moves he saw on TikTok. When I was done, I joined them."

"What happened then?" Jessie asked delicately, not wanting to interrupt the woman's stream-of-consciousness recollection.

"When Gareth got tired and stopped dancing, I went to my seat and started doing shots with Vivien," she said. "I kept waiting for Glenn to sit back down and have his drink. But he was standing up in the back talking to Gareth about something. I never even noticed Eddie sit down."

"When did you realize that it was Eddie's drink?" Valentine asked.

Lucy flinched at the memory of it.

"Not right away," she said. "When that other flight attendant started screaming, my first thought was that Eddie had a heart attack. But when Glenn went over to check on him, it started to click. I looked at the glass I'd spiked and saw that it was empty. When Glenn said that he was dead, I knew what had happened. I knew I'd killed him."

There was a tone of genuine regret in her voice.

"But you played dumb in the hangar," Jessie noted.

"What was I supposed to do, admit that I accidentally killed my old college friend when I had intended to kill my husband? I was torn up inside, thinking about Patricia having to raise her kids alone. When I mentioned that to Vivien, I meant it. But I wasn't going to confess and leave my three-year-old daughter in the care of her junkie father."

"So you stayed quiet, hoping we'd think Eddie just overdosed," Jessie said.

Lucy nodded.

"And I thought it had worked too," she said. "That is, until the girl from your station called to see if Glenn was home. I could tell from her voice that she knew something was up. And if she knew, then so did you. So I did the only thing I could."

"Make it look like Glenn committed suicide out of guilt for having killed his longtime friend?" Valentine said. "*That's* the only thing you could do?"

Lucy looked at her defiantly.

"It made sense to me. You'd have your killer. And my cheating junkie of a husband would be out of our lives forever. It was a win-win."

Lucy flinched again. Jessie thought that, like before, she was reliving a painful memory. But when she clutched her thigh, it became clear that the pain was physical. She moaned softly.

"That's it," the EMT said definitively. "We're transporting her."

They moved her to the stretcher and carried her out.

"Can you make sure she's met by officers at the hospital?" Valentine told a uniformed officer stationed outside the office. "I want her secured during her stay."

The officer nodded and got on his radio. Valentine turned back to Jessie.

"What now?" she asked.

"Now," Jessie said, feeling a little light-headed all of a sudden. "I need to sit down for a minute. I think the excitement of the last few minutes is catching up to me."

She moved over to a nearby chair in the hallway just before her legs gave out.

CHAPTER THIRTY TWO

What was that all about?" Valentine asked a few minutes later, when Jessie finally felt ready to stand up again.

"It might have something to do with performing CPR until my arms almost fell off," she answered wryly. "Or it could have been getting nearly choked to death by a woman with superhuman strength. Maybe it was just keeping non-stop pressure on the blood-soaked wound of the woman who tried to choke me to death. I'm thinking it was a combination of all of them."

"But you're better now?" Valentine wanted to know.

"I think so."

"Good," she replied excitedly, "because you should take a moment to celebrate."

"Celebrate what?"

"Well, I don't think we can do much better than we just did," Valentine said giddily, holding up her phone. "Between the recording of her confession and her attempt to kill you, I think Lucy Ward will be behind bars for quite a while."

"Yeah," Jessie said with less enthusiasm.

"What's wrong?" Valentine asked.

Jessie sighed, trying to think how best to explain it.

"I'm always happy to close a case," she finally said, "And obviously, this outcome is better than the alternative. But unfortunately, I think Lucy's worst fear could become a reality. With her in jail, little Birdie may end up in the care of a heroin addict. I hope the court considers letting her live with her grandparents, at least in the short term."

"Well, we know she'll be there for at least a few nights, considering that both her parents are in the hospital. I'll get the grandparents' number from Jamil and let them know what's up."

"Are you sure you don't want me to do that?" Jessie asked, not mentioning her concern that Valentine might not have the greatest bedside manner.

"No," she replied. "You should probably get checked out yourself, make sure your throat is okay. Your neck is looking pretty bruised there. And don't worry—I'll be sensitive when I talk to them."

"Okay, thanks," Jessie said, mildly relieved. She looked at her watch. It was 3:22. "That actually would help me a lot, because after the hospital, I've got a family thing with my sister and I want to take care of it before the end of the business day. Are you able to supervise the scene here until the sergeant and CSU get here? I can come by the station afterward to help with the paperwork."

"Don't worry about it," Valentine said. "Get your neck checked out. Do your family thing. I'll handle the paperwork. We can talk tomorrow."

"Thank you," Jessie said, and then realized she couldn't just leave it there. "And Susannah, thank you for saving my life."

"That's okay," the detective said, blushing as she looked away.

"Seriously," Jessie continued. "If not for you, there'd be a coroner's van here now. And that doesn't even account for what you did up north last night. You've had my back during this case and I really appreciate it. We have very different styles but it worked out in the end."

She still didn't really like Susannah Valentine. And she still resented the woman for her constant flirting with Ryan. But now wasn't the time to deal with that. Setting that issue aside, Jessie had to grudgingly admit that she respected her. Despite the detective's faults, she was hardworking, tough, and fearless. Those qualities had helped solve the case and save her life. For that reason alone, Valentine deserved a pass, at least for now.

"Thanks for being patient," Susannah said. "I know I can be a lot sometimes. I may have been trying a little too hard to impress you."

"What?" Jessie said, mystified. "Why would you do that?"

Susannah laughed at the question.

"Maybe because you're a living legend and I'm still trying to prove that I deserve to be in the big leagues."

Jessie shook her head, not sure how to respond.

"Come on, Jessie," Susannah said. "Even before you started profiling for the department, you were famous. You're the woman who caught the husband who tried to frame you for a murder that he committed, and then survived his attempt kill you. Then you come to LAPD, where in less than two years, much of it as a part-time consultant, you've established yourself as one of the top profilers west of the Mississippi. It's a little intimidating."

"I had no idea," Jessie said, silently noting the irony that a top notch profiler had been completely oblivious to the motivations of her partner for the last two days. "With the way you look and how you carry yourself, I didn't think you were capable of being intimidated by anyone."

"Well, you thought wrong."

The realization made Jessie wonder what else she'd been wrong about. But before she could spend too much energy worrying about that, she had another priority: the urgent meeting Dr. Lemmon had requested with her and Hannah.

In Jessie's experience, if Janice Lemmon considered something urgent, so should she.

*

"Captain Decker's insisting I take the rest of the week off from case consultation."

"I think that's a good idea too," Ryan said over the phone. "Maybe you should skip next week's seminar as well."

The light turned green and Jessie continued down the street that would get them to Dr. Lemmon's office in a couple of minutes. Sitting beside her in the passenger seat, Hannah seemed to be scrolling through her phone, but Jessie got the distinct impression that her sister was more interested in the conversation they were having.

"No way," she said. "I only have a few more weeks left before I start full-time for HSS. I'm not wasting any of them. Besides, the doctor said that I'll be completely recovered by next week. I'm just supposed to keep taking the throat spray he gave me and limit talking as much as possible over the next few days."

"That seems to be going *real* well so far," he teased.

"Be careful," she warned playfully. "Or else you might get the silent treatment for non-medical reasons."

Ryan laughed at that. The mood was light for the first time in a while and for half a second, she considered asking him if he might want to chuck the whole wedding plan and elope, as she'd mentioned to Kat. But before she could, he replied.

"What did he say about your near-fainting spell?" he asked, getting serious again. The moment for wedding talk had passed, at least for now.

"He had blood drawn as a precaution but thinks my guess was right. I exerted myself like crazy for a short period of time, and then suffered brief oxygen deprivation, all in the course of an incredibly stressful experience. He suspects I just had a delayed reaction to it and everything hit me at once."

"I hope that's all it is," Ryan said. "By the way, I'm wrapping up work at the station in the next fifteen minutes. I should be home before six. When do you think you guys will be back?"

"Not sure," Jessie said, glancing over at Hannah. "Lemmon wasn't specific about what she wanted to discuss. But I can't imagine we'll be gone too long. The woman is notorious for concluding her workday in time to get home for her 6 p.m. peppermint tea time. Considering that it's almost 5 p.m. now, we may beat you home."

"Okay," he said. "Keep me posted. I love you."

"I love you too," she replied before hanging up and turning to Hannah. "Sorry if this messes up any big dinner plans you had."

Hannah didn't say anything. In fact, other than perfunctory responses when Jessie first told her they'd be meeting with Lemmon, she'd barely spoken a word this whole time.

As Jessie pulled into the parking garage below Dr. Lemmon's building, her chest started to tighten slightly. Between Hannah's silence and Lemmon's cryptic communication, she was really starting to worry.

CHAPTER THIRTY THREE

Hannah couldn't stop fidgeting.

She'd been sitting in Dr. Lemmon's otherwise empty waiting room for ten minutes now, while she and Jessie talked in the doctor's office. Her mind ran wild at what they might be discussing.

She wasn't worried that Lemmon was telling her sister about her intentional shooting of the Night Hunter. Jessie had been there for the incident, saw it happen. She was the one who'd pleaded with Hannah to tell Lemmon in the first place.

Of course Jessie didn't know everything. She wasn't aware that her little sister had gotten a rush from committing the murder and was looking to find that high again. That was likely a topic of conversation in the office.

She tried to focus on something else and opened her phone to the recipe she'd found for roasted tomato soup. Earlier this afternoon, she'd discovered several almost-expired cans of diced tomatoes in the back of a cupboard and thought that rather than letting them go to waste, they might be a nice addition to a hearty cold-weather meal. But after realizing that she'd read the same cooking directions three times without mentally registering them, she gave up and shoved her phone in her pocket. A minute later, Dr. Lemmon opened the door.

"Would you please join us inside?" she asked, holding it wide.

Hannah got up and entered. Jessie was sitting on the couch and had left an open spot beside her, so she took it. As Dr. Lemmon returned to her chair and got settled, Hannah glanced over at her sister. She immediately knew that something was wrong.

Jessie looked stunned. Hannah had only ever seen her that way a few times, and almost every one of them involved a shocking "life or death" discovery about someone close to her. She didn't have to guess what this one was.

"Hannah," Dr. Lemmon said in a rueful tone that was rare for her. "Just now, I did something incredibly rare for me. I breached the confidentiality of our session together. I want to apologize for that."

Hannah had figured as much, and while she was pissed about it, she wasn't surprised. But she wasn't exactly sure why Lemmon seemed so repentant. It felt like another shoe was about to drop.

"Okay," she said noncommittally.

"I only do that in situations where I feel I have no other choice," Lemmon continued. "In this case, I struggled for some time before deciding how to proceed."

Hannah still didn't get what the big deal was. Jessie already knew the "how" of what she'd done that night in Wildpines. Now she apparently knew the "why" too. The revelation was undoubtedly dark and disturbing but certainly didn't seem to require such kid gloves. That is, unless—.

"Why do I feel like cops are about to burst in here?" she asked suddenly. "Am I going to be arrested? I thought you both promised me that wouldn't happen. It's the only reason I came clean. Was that all just a bunch of crap?"

"Hannah, please don't jump to conclusions—," Lemmon said calmly, which only upset her more.

"Stop trying to massage this," she demanded, her voice rising. "Am I about to get carted off to Twin Towers right now?"

"No!" Jessie blurted out, breaking her silence for the first time since Hannah came in. "You're not getting arrested, Hannah."

"Then what the hell is it?" she demanded. Her sister looked back at her helplessly so she turned to Dr. Lemmon. "What has her borderline catatonic?"

The doctor leaned in and her expression changed. Behind her thick glasses, the repentant look in her eyes was replaced by something else: sympathy mixed with firmness of purpose. Hannah didn't like it.

"While I haven't alerted the authorities, and don't intend to," Lemmon said, "I do have a professional responsibility here. When a therapist determines that a patient is a danger to themselves or to others, there is an obligation to act. Based on what you told me about the thrill you got from shooting the Night Hunter, and your desire to recapture that feeling, I have a credible concern that you might choose to act on that desire."

Hannah felt a surge of white hot anger erupt in her chest. Just as she'd feared, the secret she'd been afraid to reveal was being used against her. The people she'd trusted had betrayed her. She tried to keep a lid on her fury, knowing it would only reinforce their concerns.

"But I *didn't* act on it," she reminded them forcefully. "The incident happened over a month ago and I haven't done anything since. In fact, all I've done since then is try to get a handle on it by talking to *you*. And now you're going to use that against me?"

"That's not my intent, Hannah," Dr. Lemmon insisted, "but you have to acknowledge that you've been chasing that feeling again. You mentioned to me just a few weeks ago that you imagined jamming a broken wine bottle into the jugular of a teen bully in a convenience store."

"Right," Hannah countered. "But I didn't do it, did I? Instead, I shamed him using these things called 'words.' Isn't that what a non-murderous person does? And then I told you about it. Doesn't that show that I'm trying to get a handle on this thing? Are you going to punish me for being honest?"

"Of course not," Lemmon assured her. "I'm going to help you. And I think I may have found a way to do that. That's why we're all here now. That's why I wanted to speak to Jessie first, to see if my idea seemed plausible to her. And after some discussion, we both think that it might be a way to help you while keeping the people around you safe."

Hannah looked at her sister, who for the first time ever, appeared completely lost. She returned her attention to Lemmon.

"Keep them safe?" she shot back. "What do you think I'm going to do? Slice her throat in the middle of the night? Slice Ryan's? If I wanted to do that, I've had plenty of chances. I don't want to hurt them. I love them. I love Jessie. She's my sister. She's the only person I have left."

She heard her voice crack at that last line and hated herself for it.

"I know you love her," Dr. Lemmon soothed. "And I'm not suggesting you would ever hurt her. That's not who I'm talking about."

"Who then?"

"The other people around you all the time, Hannah," Lemmon explained. "I'm talking about bullies in stores, or drug dealers in parks, or anyone you judge unworthy and decide deserves your brand of punishment."

Hannah shook her head in frustration.

"I shot a serial killer who slaughtered hundreds of people, Dr. Lemmon," she pleaded. "I know he wasn't a threat at that point and that it was wrong. But it's not like I'm going around killing everybody I find morally lacking. I just fantasize about it occasionally. Haven't you ever had thoughts like that?"

"I think we can both agree that these are more than just abstract fantasies, Hannah," Lemmon said. "The way you described it reminded me of my patients with addictions, the ones who won't go to rehab and are trying to get by white knuckling it through every day. I hate to tell you this, but almost all of them relapsed."

"So what are you saying exactly?" Hannah snarled, "That I should go to murderer rehab?"

Dr. Lemmon exchanged a look with Jessie, who seemed to have finally found her bearings again. She nodded at Lemmon, who answered.

"In a way, yes," she said mildly. "I think—and your sister has agreed—that you could be well-served by spending some time in a residential psychiatric facility, where you can work on tackling these urges in a structured environment."

Now Hannah understood why her sister had looked so stunned earlier. That's how she felt now.

"You want to lock me up in a psycho ward?" she croaked disbelievingly.

"Absolutely not," Lemmon said firmly. "We'd like you to check yourself in voluntarily. We want you to be a part of this process from day one, to have a say in your treatment. I have a specific facility in mind. It's where I recommend my patients with suicidal ideation go; same for those who have life-threatening eating disorders. I even had a patient with uncontrolled OCD go there. It's not primarily a lockdown facility, although they do have a secure wing. But that's not what I envision for you."

"What do you 'envision' for me?" Hannah asked sarcastically.

The doctor ignored her tone.

"I'm taking about intense therapy sessions, both group and individual, some of which I would be involved in. I'm talking about exploring brain-mapping, redirection therapy, anything we think might work. So in a way, it is a kind of rehab."

"What do you mean?" Hannah demanded through gritted teeth. She was trying her best to be mature about this but the churning in her belly was making it difficult.

"The goal is to re-wire your brain," Lemmon clarified, "like we would with an alcoholic or a drug or sex addict, so they have some weapons to battle the self-defeating behaviors that can contribute to their illness. The only difference—and I'll admit that it's a big one—is that your addiction seems to center around wanting to kill people. And we can't treat that in a traditional rehab center. Plus, I couldn't guarantee you the kind of confidentiality you'd need there. Someone might report what was said and that *could* put you at legal risk."

"You think someone would call TMZ?" Hannah wondered half-jokingly.

"It's not inconceivable," Lemmon replied without smiling. "But at this facility, everything you reveal in a therapeutic setting is protected by privilege, which is why I'm hoping you'll check yourself in voluntarily. The very act of doing that, of choosing to be there, and actively pursuing help, is a *prima facie* indicator that you're not a threat to others, or at least that you don't want to be."

"I see," Hannah replied, not sure what the proper response was.

She knew the response she *wanted* to give and it wasn't verbal. When she first walked into the office earlier, she'd noticed a letter opener on Dr. Lemmon's desk, resting beside several newly opened envelopes.

She pictured herself leaping up, grabbing it, and plunging it upward into the psychiatrist's throat, shoving it hard until it reached her brain stem. There was no way that Jessie, recovering from the altercation with her suspect this afternoon, could stop her in time. She imagined the blood spurting everywhere, covering both her and her sister, who would arrive moments too late to help.

She, to use Lemmon's word, "envisioned" the doctor's wide-eyed expression of horror as, in her moment of death, she comprehended that she'd both over *and* underestimated the final patient she would ever see. Hannah's fingers actually twitched as she visualized picking up the metal tool. It was so close. It would be so easy.

"What do you think?" Jessie asked, tearing her out of her fantasy, "Are you willing to try this?"

Hannah looked at her sister. Jessie was clearly exhausted, both physically and emotionally. Her eyes were rimmed with tears on the precipice of rolling down her cheeks. It occurred to Hannah that that they were both white knuckling it these days.

She didn't want that for the person who had saved her when her life was spinning out of control. Jessie was already traumatized enough. Did Hannah really want to be another source of suffering for someone who'd opened her home and her heart to a virtual stranger and embraced her as a real sister?

And the truth was that after the letter opener scenario she'd just hungrily played out in her head, she was scared. What would she have done if Jessie had interrupted her violent daydream a few seconds later? Hannah knew in her heart what she would have done. And that convinced her that she really did need help. She looked at Dr. Lemmon.

"You think this could work?" she asked.

The doctor shrugged.

"I can't promise you anything," she replied. "But I think it might. And isn't that better than what you're doing now?"

Hannah sighed deeply before responding.

"Okay," she finally said. "Let's do it."

EPILOGUE

Eden Roth giggled as she watched the scene.

Clueless was her favorite movie. That's why she'd seen it 822 times. That included every night for the last eight months, ever since her release from the Female Forensic In-Patient Psychiatric Unit at the Twin Towers Correctional Facility. It was part of her ritual. It soothed her.

Every night when she got home from work, she followed the same routine. First, she did a thorough dusting of her tiny apartment. Then she changed into her footie pajamas, even if it was hot out and she sweated through them. After that, she made dinner, which was always a baked potato with bacon bits, chives, and butter. She prepared it while she watched the local news, so she could stay abreast of what was happening in her community.

Then she settled into her comfy chair and started the movie for the 823rd time. She'd watch until Cher's dad told her that "everywhere in L.A. takes twenty minutes," and then pause the movie. It was the perfect time because she was always done with her potato by that point, and also because Cher's dad was a dirty liar.

It took way more than twenty minutes to get to some places in L.A. and Mel Horowitz had to know that. She'd scrub her plate aggressively, using the activity to get her energy out until her anger with Mr. Horowitz had subsided. Then she would get herself a small scoop of mint chocolate chip ice cream, put it in a bowl, and settle in for the rest of the movie.

Just before she hit play, she would double check that her phone was charged, just in case she got the call. Even though it had yet to come in the last eight months, she knew it eventually would, and she wanted to be prepared. She owed that to Andrea Robinson and to the Principles.

After all, when she'd first entered Twin Towers, it was Andy who had taken her under her wing. It was Andy who'd shown her that she was more than just a shy wallflower with crazy dreams. And unlike the others in lockup, Andy never made fun of her when she learned what she'd done to end up there.

Eden liked to cut herself, sometimes on her palms, sometimes on her forearms and then rub the blood on her hands. Then she would walk through busy L.A. tourist areas, hugging people, smearing them with her life force.

It was just her way of trying to make the world brighter and more colorful. But the people she painted with her blood didn't like it. And neither did the legal system, Andy didn't think it was that big a deal. She had said it was lovely, that Eden was trying to add some beauty to the world, and that the powers that be just wanted to keep everything drab and gray.

But Andy also explained that unless she stopped cutting herself and rubbing others with her blood, she'd never get out of Twin Towers and back to watching *Clueless*. And then Andy told her about the Principles. They changed her life.

After that day, Eden was on her best behavior. She didn't cut herself once in prison. She said all the right things—the things Andy told her to say—in therapy. And once they let her out, she got a job as a cashier at a dollar store. Andy said she needed a job with a manager she reported to regularly, one who could tell the authorities that she was doing well and not causing trouble. She was what Andy called a "model citizen."

It wasn't perfect. She hadn't spoken to her family in years, not since the night her stepdad had touched her in the bad way one time too many and she had to use the scissors on him a lot and then run away. And no, she didn't have any friends, unless she counted Cher Horowitz, Dionne, and Tai. And of course she had Andy. There was always Andy.

She was just settling in with her ice cream, enjoying Cher quote *Hamlet* and embarrass Josh's mean girlfriend, when her phone rang. She paused the movie and looked at the caller ID. She didn't recognize the number but that didn't matter. She'd been told she should always answer, just in case. So she did.

"This is Eden."

"Oh, I'm sorry," the woman on the other end of the line said. "I thought I was calling Three Man Pizza. I must have the wrong number. Are you sure this isn't Three Man Pizza?"

"Yes, I'm sure," Eden replied, offering the pre-arranged response she'd practiced so many times in the bathroom mirror. "This isn't Three Man Pizza. But I'm sure you'll find what you're looking for."

"Thank you. I hope so," the other woman said, then hung up.

That was it. After all this time, she'd finally gotten the call. She'd been activated. Standing up, she walked quickly to the bathroom mirror. There was a bit of ice cream on her upper lip. She licked it up with her tongue. Then she stared at herself.

Eden knew she wasn't pretty. Her stepdad had told her that many times, even though he seemed to like her looks enough to do those things to her. But she knew he was right. That was why people walked by her without ever looking at her. That's why they sometimes didn't hear her when she talked.

She was short and skinny, without curves. Her brown hair was limp. Her skin was pale but not in an elegant way. Her eyes were gray and dull. She just wasn't memorable.

But that was about to change. Andy had promised her that once she got the call and accepted the mission, she would be remembered forever, as long as she stuck to the Principles. Andy was counting on her. Eden wouldn't let her down.

It was time to get to work.

THE PERFECT RUMOR
(A Jessie Hunt Psychological Suspense Thriller—Book Nineteen)

A wealthy husband is found murdered at a fabulous cliffside Palos Verdes spa resort, while vacationing with his wife. Amidst the massive guest villas, couples' massages, and chef-prepared meals, Jessie realizes that not all is as perfect as it seems. It is only perfect for a murder.

"A masterpiece of thriller and mystery. Blake Pierce did a magnificent job developing characters with a psychological side so well described that we feel inside their minds, follow their fears and cheer for their success. Full of twists, this book will keep you awake until the turn of the last page."
--Books and Movie Reviews, Roberto Mattos (re *Once Gone*)

THE PERFECT RUMOR is book #19 in a new psychological suspense series by bestselling author Blake Pierce, which begins with *The Perfect Wife*, a #1 bestseller (and free download) with over 5,000 five-star ratings and 900 five-star reviews.

Rumors abound amongst the uber wealthy in this VIP-only resort, nestled in ostentatious surroundings: oceanside yoga, meditation hikes, catered picnics, and personal "couples' lovemaking" coaches. All is seemingly too perfect, Jessie knows.

But the victim had no apparent enemies.

Who would want him dead? And why?

A fast-paced psychological suspense thriller with unforgettable characters and heart-pounding suspense, THE JESSIE HUNT series is a riveting new series that will leave you turning pages late into the night.

Books #20 and #21 in the series—THE PERFECT COUPLE and THE PERFECT MURDER—are now also available.

Blake Pierce

Blake Pierce is the USA Today bestselling author of the RILEY PAGE mystery series, which includes seventeen books. Blake Pierce is also the author of the MACKENZIE WHITE mystery series, comprising fourteen books; of the AVERY BLACK mystery series, comprising six books; of the KERI LOCKE mystery series, comprising five books; of the MAKING OF RILEY PAIGE mystery series, comprising six books; of the KATE WISE mystery series, comprising seven books; of the CHLOE FINE psychological suspense mystery, comprising six books; of the JESSE HUNT psychological suspense thriller series, comprising nineteen books; of the AU PAIR psychological suspense thriller series, comprising three books; of the ZOE PRIME mystery series, comprising six books; of the ADELE SHARP mystery series, comprising thirteen books, of the EUROPEAN VOYAGE cozy mystery series, comprising four books; of the new LAURA FROST FBI suspense thriller, comprising six books (and counting); of the new ELLA DARK FBI suspense thriller, comprising nine books (and counting); of the A YEAR IN EUROPE cozy mystery series, comprising nine books, of the AVA GOLD mystery series, comprising six books (and counting); and of the RACHEL GIFT mystery series, comprising six books (and counting).

An avid reader and lifelong fan of the mystery and thriller genres, Blake loves to hear from you, so please feel free to visit www.blakepierceauthor.com to learn more and stay in touch.

.

BOOKS BY BLAKE PIERCE

RACHEL GIFT MYSTERY SERIES
HER LAST WISH (Book #1)
HER LAST CHANCE (Book #2)
HER LAST HOPE (Book #3)
HER LAST FEAR (Book #4)
HER LAST CHOICE (Book #5)
HER LAST BREATH (Book #6)

AVA GOLD MYSTERY SERIES
CITY OF PREY (Book #1)
CITY OF FEAR (Book #2)
CITY OF BONES (Book #3)
CITY OF GHOSTS (Book #4)
CITY OF DEATH (Book #5)
CITY OF VICE (Book #6)

A YEAR IN EUROPE
A MURDER IN PARIS (Book #1)
DEATH IN FLORENCE (Book #2)
VENGEANCE IN VIENNA (Book #3)
A FATALITY IN SPAIN (Book #4)

ELLA DARK FBI SUSPENSE THRILLER
GIRL, ALONE (Book #1)
GIRL, TAKEN (Book #2)
GIRL, HUNTED (Book #3)
GIRL, SILENCED (Book #4)
GIRL, VANISHED (Book 5)
GIRL ERASED (Book #6)
GIRL, FORSAKEN (Book #7)
GIRL, TRAPPED (Book #8)
GIRL, EXPENDABLE (Book #9)

LAURA FROST FBI SUSPENSE THRILLER
ALREADY GONE (Book #1)
ALREADY SEEN (Book #2)
ALREADY TRAPPED (Book #3)
ALREADY MISSING (Book #4)

ALREADY DEAD (Book #5)
ALREADY TAKEN (Book #6)

EUROPEAN VOYAGE COZY MYSTERY SERIES
MURDER (AND BAKLAVA) (Book #1)
DEATH (AND APPLE STRUDEL) (Book #2)
CRIME (AND LAGER) (Book #3)
MISFORTUNE (AND GOUDA) (Book #4)
CALAMITY (AND A DANISH) (Book #5)
MAYHEM (AND HERRING) (Book #6)

ADELE SHARP MYSTERY SERIES
LEFT TO DIE (Book #1)
LEFT TO RUN (Book #2)
LEFT TO HIDE (Book #3)
LEFT TO KILL (Book #4)
LEFT TO MURDER (Book #5)
LEFT TO ENVY (Book #6)
LEFT TO LAPSE (Book #7)
LEFT TO VANISH (Book #8)
LEFT TO HUNT (Book #9)
LEFT TO FEAR (Book #10)
LEFT TO PREY (Book #11)
LEFT TO LURE (Book #12)
LEFT TO CRAVE (Book #13)

THE AU PAIR SERIES
ALMOST GONE (Book#1)
ALMOST LOST (Book #2)
ALMOST DEAD (Book #3)

ZOE PRIME MYSTERY SERIES
FACE OF DEATH (Book#1)
FACE OF MURDER (Book #2)
FACE OF FEAR (Book #3)
FACE OF MADNESS (Book #4)
FACE OF FURY (Book #5)
FACE OF DARKNESS (Book #6)

A JESSIE HUNT PSYCHOLOGICAL SUSPENSE SERIES

THE PERFECT WIFE (Book #1)
THE PERFECT BLOCK (Book #2)
THE PERFECT HOUSE (Book #3)
THE PERFECT SMILE (Book #4)
THE PERFECT LIE (Book #5)
THE PERFECT LOOK (Book #6)
THE PERFECT AFFAIR (Book #7)
THE PERFECT ALIBI (Book #8)
THE PERFECT NEIGHBOR (Book #9)
THE PERFECT DISGUISE (Book #10)
THE PERFECT SECRET (Book #11)
THE PERFECT FAÇADE (Book #12)
THE PERFECT IMPRESSION (Book #13)
THE PERFECT DECEIT (Book #14)
THE PERFECT MISTRESS (Book #15)
THE PERFECT IMAGE (Book #16)
THE PERFECT VEIL (Book #17)
THE PERFECT INDISCRETION (Book #18)
THE PERFECT RUMOR (Book #19)

CHLOE FINE PSYCHOLOGICAL SUSPENSE SERIES
NEXT DOOR (Book #1)
A NEIGHBOR'S LIE (Book #2)
CUL DE SAC (Book #3)
SILENT NEIGHBOR (Book #4)
HOMECOMING (Book #5)
TINTED WINDOWS (Book #6)

KATE WISE MYSTERY SERIES
IF SHE KNEW (Book #1)
IF SHE SAW (Book #2)
IF SHE RAN (Book #3)
IF SHE HID (Book #4)
IF SHE FLED (Book #5)
IF SHE FEARED (Book #6)
IF SHE HEARD (Book #7)

THE MAKING OF RILEY PAIGE SERIES
WATCHING (Book #1)
WAITING (Book #2)

LURING (Book #3)
TAKING (Book #4)
STALKING (Book #5)
KILLING (Book #6)

RILEY PAIGE MYSTERY SERIES
ONCE GONE (Book #1)
ONCE TAKEN (Book #2)
ONCE CRAVED (Book #3)
ONCE LURED (Book #4)
ONCE HUNTED (Book #5)
ONCE PINED (Book #6)
ONCE FORSAKEN (Book #7)
ONCE COLD (Book #8)
ONCE STALKED (Book #9)
ONCE LOST (Book #10)
ONCE BURIED (Book #11)
ONCE BOUND (Book #12)
ONCE TRAPPED (Book #13)
ONCE DORMANT (Book #14)
ONCE SHUNNED (Book #15)
ONCE MISSED (Book #16)
ONCE CHOSEN (Book #17)

MACKENZIE WHITE MYSTERY SERIES
BEFORE HE KILLS (Book #1)
BEFORE HE SEES (Book #2)
BEFORE HE COVETS (Book #3)
BEFORE HE TAKES (Book #4)
BEFORE HE NEEDS (Book #5)
BEFORE HE FEELS (Book #6)
BEFORE HE SINS (Book #7)
BEFORE HE HUNTS (Book #8)
BEFORE HE PREYS (Book #9)
BEFORE HE LONGS (Book #10)
BEFORE HE LAPSES (Book #11)
BEFORE HE ENVIES (Book #12)
BEFORE HE STALKS (Book #13)
BEFORE HE HARMS (Book #14)